MR. & MRS. SMITH

NOW A MAJOR MOTION PICTURE

RELEASED BY TWENTIETH CENTURY FOX

STARRING

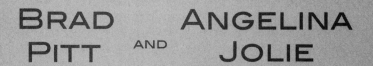

BRAD PITT AND ANGELINA JOLIE

BY JANE AND JOHN SMITH AS TOLD TO DR. MARK WEXLER

BASED ON THE MOTION PICTURE SCREENPLAY BY

SIMON KINBERG AND KIERAN AND MICHELLE MULRONEY

PERENNIAL CURRENTS

AN IMPRINT OF HARPERCOLLINS PUBLISHERS

MR. & MRS. SMITH

HarperCollins books may be purchased for educational, business,
or sales promotional use. For information please write: Special Markets
Department, HarperCollins Publishers Inc., 10 East 53rd Street,
New York, NY 10022.

FIRST EDITION

Designed by Chris Welch

*Photographs copyright © 2005 by
Twentieth Century Fox Film Corporation.*

Library of Congress Cataloging-in-Publication Data

Dubowski, Cathy East.
    Mr. and Mrs. Smith / Cathy East Dubowski.—1st ed.
        p. cm.
    Novelization of the Twentieth Century Fox motion picture screenplay
written by Simon Kinberg.
        ISBN 0-06-075862-7 (trade pbk.)
        1. Married people—Fiction. 2. Murder for hire—Fiction.
3. Assassins—Fiction. I. Kinberg, Simon. II. Title.

PS3554.U2637M7 2005
813'.54—dc22   2004060098

05 06 07 08 09 WBC/RRD 10 9 8 7 6 5 4 3 2 1

For Dr. Wexler,
With eternal gratitude for
the oil check.

—Jane and John Smith

For Dr. Wexler,
With eternal gratitude for
the oil check.

—*Jane and John Smith*

ACKNOWLEDGMENTS

This book was a labor of love, as well as a collaborative effort, and so I send my affections and gratitude to all those who helped make this book possible:

To my wonderful editor, Hope Innelli, at HarperCollins, for her encouragement, good humor, and brilliant editorial guidance—and for giving me "hope" when I felt as if I would never finish this book!

To Casey Kait, also at HarperCollins, for her cheerful e-mails and phone calls when deadlines loomed.

To Debbie Olshan, at Twentieth Century Fox, for taking every twist and turn in the adventure with us—I can't wait to see the movie!

To my assistant, Katrina Östlicher—typist extraordinaire and human spellchecker—who spent endless hours compiling my endless notes and transcripts. What would I do without you?

To Cathy, my oldest friend, who is always there for me—thanks for all the late-night sessions!

And last but not least, to Jane and John for sharing their inspiring story. Good luck with all your new adventures, and remember: My door is always open if you ever need to stop by for another "Oil Check."
               —M.W.

DR. WEXLER

Katrina—is the tape on?

Okay, yes. Hand me the mike. This is Dr. Wexler, and these are the transcripts from my taped sessions with a Mr. and Mrs. John Smith from the first of last month. Compiled and typed up by my assistant, Katrina Östlicher. Also includes comments typed in from my notes about the patients' facial expressions, body language, etc., etc., as usual, and so on.

When Mr. and Mrs. Smith enter my office, I am somewhat surprised. First of all, they are a bit younger than the couples I usually see. Very nice looking, too. Like movie stars, actually, both of them. Well groomed, neatly dressed. Polite.

Both seem quite pleasant, very intelligent.

And they are smiling.

To look at them, you'd think they were the perfect couple.

So, Mr. and Mrs. Smith, I think, *what are you doing in a marriage counselor's office?*

Sometimes my clients storm into my office in a bloody rage. Sometimes they come in quiet—volcanoes about to erupt. Sometimes you can tell they've even been arguing in the waiting room. Ach! The things my receptionist tells me! I could write a book!

But these two. No clue. They are, if not overly affectionate in public, extremely polite with each other. I note that he even holds out her chair for her. And she says, "Thank you."

Very unusual, in my office.

I am instantly intrigued.

I've been in practice almost twenty-three years, and I've seen just about everything you can imagine. But in general, most people fall into a few predictable categories. Husband cheated on wife with another woman. Wife cheated on husband with another man. Or another woman. Wife more successful in her career than husband, and so on.

But I sense something different going on with Mr. and Mrs. Smith. And so, I think, an interesting case.

As usual, I ask permission to record their session. What follows below is the taped session, transcribed verbatim to paper, interspersed with my notes and observations.

FIRST SESSION, MR. AND MRS. SMITH

I allow Mr. and Mrs. Smith to settle into their seats. I smile at them over my glasses, then spend a few moments offering them coffee or tea (both decline), opening their file, selecting a pen from my pen holder, polishing my glasses—a technique that allows my clients a chance to settle in and relax before I ask the first question.

NOTE: Mr. Smith is already leaning forward, anxious to make something clear.

MR. SMITH: "Okay. First up, I want to say we don't really need to be here—"

NOTE: Yes. A lot of people begin this way.

MRS. SMITH (smiling): "Actually it's a funny story."

MR. SMITH (chuckling): "We were at a charity event, a church auction slash barbecue—"

MRS. SMITH: "—our friends the Colemans. They live next door. Devout—"

MR. SMITH: "Episcopalians."

MRS. SMITH: "Presbyterians."

NOTE: *Slight discrepancy. Nothing to worry about. Unless . . . ah, yes. A little frown passes between them.*

MR. SMITH: "Anyway, the grand lot was—"

MRS. SMITH: "—a mystery lot."

MR. SMITH: "I'd sunk a few, wasn't driving—"

MRS. SMITH: "A few?"

NOTE: *Mrs. Smith rolls eyes. Mr. Smith responds with a hard look. A muscle twitches along his jaw. Obviously his drinking is an issue.*

But he doesn't take the bait.

Classic case of withholding his feelings. At least in front of strangers.

My early guess is that this is a couple who never argue in public.

Mr. Smith continues as if he hasn't been interrupted.

MR. SMITH: "So Jane starts bidding. She gets a *tiny bit* competitive . . ."

NOTE: *Mrs. Smith's lips purse at this remark. Another issue between them?*

MR. SMITH: "Upshot is: We end up blowing eight hundred bucks on the mystery lot."

MR. AND MRS. SMITH (at once): "Four sessions with Dr. Wexler."

NOTE: *They both laugh. Politely. A little too loudly.*

MR. SMITH: "The Colemans have a great sense of humor."

NOTE: *Another burst of laughter, which fades quickly.*

Now my senses are on alert. The couple hasn't come here on their own initiative.

And yet they came.

I scratch out a note, giving them time, to make sure they've said their piece.

Then I look up at them and smile.

ME: "But you didn't have to come."

NOTE: Complete silence.

Mr. and Mrs. Smith glance at each other, then quickly look away.

I say nothing, and wait patiently. Sometimes it's the best way to get someone to talk. A comfortable silence doesn't bother a person whose mind is at ease. But a pregnant pause seems to compel people who are nervous to completely spill their guts.

It's a little technique I picked up from police dramas on TV.

I wait.

MR. SMITH: "Right—"

MRS. SMITH: "Absolutely."

NOTE: They sit back in their chairs. A bit nervous. I can see Mrs. Smith thinking, though.

MRS. SMITH: "But we have a theory . . ."

MR. SMITH (startled): "We do?"

MRS. SMITH (smiling): "The 'Oil Check.'"

MR. SMITH: "Oh. *Right.*"

Note: I have the distinct impression that this is the first time Mr. Smith has heard about this theory. But he's playing along.

MR. SMITH: "See, we've been married five years—"

MRS. SMITH: "Six."

MR. SMITH: "—five, six years, and this is like a checkup for us. A chance to peek around the engine, maybe change the oil, replace a seal or two."

NOTE: How many years married seems to be an issue.

Mr. Smith seems really into the auto-mechanic analogy.

Mr. and Mrs. Smith smile at each other, then turn back to me. The perfect happy couple.

They remind me of another perfect couple. Barbie and Ken.

I begin to see where this might be heading.

ME (smiling): "Very well, then. Let's pop the hood.

"Please answer the following questions as quickly and instinctively as possible."

MRS. SMITH: "Sure."

MR. SMITH (gesturing like a gunslinger): "From the hip."

ME: "On a scale of one to ten, how happy are you as a couple?"

MRS. SMITH: "Eight."

MR. SMITH: "Wait."

NOTE: Mrs. Smith has spoken instantly. Mr. Smith seems startled by her answer.

MR. SMITH: "So, like ten being perfectly happy and one being . . . totally miserable?"

ME: "Just answer instinctively."

MR. SMITH: "Okay. Ready?"

MRS. SMITH: "Ready."

MR. AND MRS. SMITH (at once): "Eight."

NOTE: Interesting . . . not too hot, not too cold. Like porridge.

ME (next card): "On a scale of one to ten, how happy would you say your partner is?"

MR. SMITH: "Eight."

NOTE: This time it's Mr. Smith who has the instant answer, Mrs. Smith who hesitates.

MRS. SMITH: "Um, are we allowed fractions?"

NOTE: Mr. Smith seems taken aback by her answer and leans over.

ME AND MR. SMITH (at the same time): "It's what's instinctive."

MRS. SMITH: "Okay, I'm all set. One, two, three . . ."

MR. AND MRS. SMITH (at once): "Eight."

NOTE: Eight again. They look at me for approval, as if I am their teacher and they are answering questions at the blackboard.

Very interesting . . . Eight is a very telling number. Safe cruising altitude. No drama—high or low. No passion one way or the other.

Now that I've warmed them up, time for the Big One. I glance down at my card, my face impassive so as not to give away what's to come.

The shock value usually provokes the truest response.

ME (casually): "How often do you have sex?"

NOTE: I have to glance back up to make sure they are still there.

They are, but they look like a picture postcard. Stunned. A little shell-shocked.

MRS. SMITH (blushing): "I . . . don't understand the question."

NOTE: Yes, you do, Mrs. Smith.

MR. SMITH (squirming in chair): "Wait. Okay, I'm lost. Is this a one-to-ten thing?"

NOTE: Ah, Mr. Smith. Quit stalling.

MRS. SMITH: "Right. I mean, because if it is, does one equal 'not much' or is one like, 'nothing.' Because strictly speaking, zero should be nothing."

MR. SMITH: "Exactly. Plus, if we don't know what one is, what's ten?"

MRS. SMITH: "Right . . . Is ten . . . you know . . ."

MR. SMITH: "Constant . . . unrelenting . . ."

MRS. SMITH: "Twenty-four/seven . . . without a break. For anything."

MR. SMITH: "Not even to eat."

MRS. SMITH: "Like Sting."

MR. SMITH: "Exactly."

NOTE: Mr. Smith shakes head emphatically—he's found a well-known figure upon which to divert our attention—a tactic that can help alleviate his feelings of guilt or discomfort.

MR. SMITH: "Look at Sting's day job. Who else has sixty hours a week to put aside in the sack?"

NOTE: Okay, I think I'm ready to hazard a guess here. Based on my professional instincts and experience, I write down a number. My estimate of how often this young couple has had sex in the last month. Maybe the whole year.

ME (calmly, nonjudgmental): "This is not a one-to-ten scenario. It's a straight question."

NOTE: I wait for them to settle down a little. It is, after all, an embarrassing question to answer in front of a stranger. Some people just say they can't remember. Sometimes people boast. Often they flat-out lie.

I wait for the Smiths to speak. And when no one does, I ask the question again.

ME (clearing my throat): "How often do you have sex?"

NOTE: Still no answer.

ME (prodding): "How about this week?"

MR. SMITH (stalling again): "Including the weekend?"

ME (shrugging, smiling reassuringly): "Sure."

NOTE: Mr. Smith sinks back in his chair and stares at his hands. Mrs. Smith seems to be studying the pattern in my office curtains.

Ah, Mr. and Mrs. Smith. Can't even say the number out loud, can you.

But then I guess they don't really have to.

I retrace the number I've written down in my notes—a nice round even number.

Zero.

Then I check my calendar to see if I can get them back in early next week.

I think we have a lot of work to do.

SECOND SESSION, MR. AND MRS. SMITH

NOTE: Clients fail to show.

Mrs. Smith calls later, apologizing. Says something came up. Declines to reschedule. Says she has to check with her husband. Will call back later.

An hour later Mr. Smith calls, apologizing. Says he had to go out of town unexpectedly. Declines to reschedule. Says he has to check with his wife. Will call back later.

Mrs. Smith calls the next day.

Wonders if she can come in on Tuesday.

By herself.

Interesting . . .

SECOND SESSION, MRS. SMITH, ALONE

Mrs. Smith, second session. Full transcript of our recorded conversation, with my notes added.

Mrs. Smith comes in, hesitant, apologetic. Sits down, crosses legs. Uncrosses legs. Leans forward. Leans back. Twists her wedding ring repeatedly.

The woman looks tired. I check my notes: Mrs. Smith runs a computer temp agency. Does a lot of on-site troubleshooting for major companies in the city. Hours erratic, sometimes middle-of-the-night calls. Travels a lot, no kids. A busy schedule.

But her exhaustion seems more than physical. I sense a deep emotional fatigue. She has a dazzling smile, but it doesn't quite reach her eyes. Her eyes look tired. Empty. Sad.

I do my usual paper shuffling, waiting for her to relax. I offer her coffee, tea, she declines. But she does ask if she can smoke.

I'm surprised; she didn't smoke at the first session. Maybe not in front of her husband? A little secret perhaps?

I tell her of course she can smoke. I don't encourage smoking, but as a former smoker myself, I know that a cigarette can help a person relax in this kind of session. It's important at this stage that she not feel judged in any way.

Perhaps we can work on the smoking later.

But for now, we'll deal with the marriage.

She slips a cigarette out from a lovely leather case in her bag and lights it with a matching lighter. There is a glamour about *this gesture that makes Mrs. Smith seem sexier than I recall—more like an actress from those old black-and-white movies. You know the classic thrillers, Like Dial M for Murder. The impression is strikingly different from the one she made on her first visit. As she takes a long drag on her cigarette she becomes visibly more relaxed.*

Now we can begin.

ME: "Tell me, Mrs. Smith. Why did you decide to come back alone?"

MRS. SMITH (shrugs, looks away): "I'm not sure, really. I don't think we have a problem. I mean, I love my husband, love my house, love our life . . ."

NOTE: She doesn't complete the sentence. There's a big but hanging unsaid in the air. Whatever it is, she can't seem to make herself continue.

ME (prodding): "But . . . ?"

NOTE: Mrs. Smith's eyes take on a faraway look. She's obviously replaying scenes in her mind, things that make her sad.

Then she just shrugs.

ME: "And yet . . . you're here. Alone. This is no longer a charity door prize that you've cashed in on a whim . . . It's not really an 'oil check,' is it, Mrs. Smith?"

NOTE: Mrs. Smith looks at her hands, shakes her head.

ME: "So obviously you feel a need to talk about something."

NOTE: Forced smile. I rephrase my question.

ME: "So what do you think the problem is?"

NOTE: Mrs. Smith smokes and looks out the window. I sense that she is a woman who keeps everything inside. It will not be easy for her to share her innermost feelings. Especially out loud.

At last she turns back to me.

MRS. SMITH: "There's this space between us, and it keeps filling up with everything we don't say to each other. What's that called?"

ME (wryly): "Marriage."

NOTE: Mrs. Smith considers, takes another puff of her cigarette.

MRS. SMITH: "He has this way of being right there in a room, and just being . . . gone."

ME: "Can you give me an example?"

NOTE: The tape stopped here. But she mentioned a few things. An argument over curtains. Lack of conversation at the dinner table . . . Something about passing the salt, little skirmishes over whose side of the table it's on . . .

The kind of things that aren't important.

And yet they are. Not because they're important in and of themselves: table manners and home decorating and who sleeps on what side of the bed.

But they're important because they're symptoms: They can become tiny battlegrounds for the unspoken problems that even the participants themselves don't fully understand and can't express.

While I fiddle with my tape recorder, I let her talk until she runs out of things to say.

She looks troubled, frustrated. She knows she's having difficulty expressing what's wrong.

NOTE: Taping again.

ME: "How honest are you with your husband?"

NOTE: Mrs. Smith looks like a deer caught in the headlights of an oncoming truck.

She takes another drag on her cigarette. Blows it out slowly. Eyes wandering.

MRS. SMITH: "Pretty honest . . . Not that I lie to him. Just that . . . I'm sure we both keep little secrets.

"Everybody keeps little secrets, right?"

NOTE: I shrug, nonjudgmental. My sense is that Mrs. Smith is keeping quite a few things secret from her husband. Perhaps even something important.

ME: "Mrs. Smith, I'm going to give you a little homework."

NOTE: She laughs nervously.

ME: "Nothing to worry about, I assure you. I want you to go home and write about your feelings."

MRS. SMITH: "Oh, well. I'm not much of a writer, Dr. Wexler. And my job . . . I'm awfully busy, and . . ."

ME: "I understand. But you don't need to worry. This is not a school assignment for your English teacher. It doesn't have to be polished. It doesn't even have to be in complete sentences. And no one has to see it but you. You don't have to show it to anyone."

MRS. SMITH: "Not even you?"

ME: "Not even me. Of course, you can show it to me if you like. But mostly it's to help you open up to yourself so you can begin to understand what's really troubling you. Sometimes we don't know what our story is until we tell it to ourselves."

NOTE: Mrs. Smith smokes, thinking.

MRS. SMITH: "Nobody has to see it."

ME: "Nobody."

MRS. SMITH: "Not even . . . John."

ME: "Not even John."

MRS. SMITH (shrugs): "I'll try."

ME: "Excellent! I think it will really be helpful."

MRS. SMITH: "Um. Does it matter what kind of notebook, or pen—"

ME (smiling reassuringly): "Doesn't matter."

MRS. SMITH: "Um . . . How should I begin?"

ME: "Why don't you begin at the beginning? Write about how you met. Try to remember why you fell in love with your husband in the first place . . ."

NOTE: Mrs. Smith gazes out the window. At last a smile. A lovely one, in fact. She is remembering something extremely pleasant.

MRS. SMITH: "It was in Colombia. Bogotá. Six years ago . . ."

NOTE: I nod, pleased. I can tell from her face . . . there are still a few embers smoldering among the ashes of this marriage.

ME (encouraging): "Very good. Begin with that. Oh, I do wish we could get Mr. Smith to do this, too. Do you think it's a possibility—"

MRS. SMITH (looks stricken): "Oh, no! I mean, I don't think he wants to come in anymore. I mean, well, you know how men are. He's not really into . . . things like this. And actually, well . . ."

ME: "Yes?"

MRS. SMITH (soft laugh): "I haven't exactly mentioned to him—yet—that I was coming alone. I didn't want to worry him, you know. Or make him think I thought there was something really wrong. I just sort of wanted . . . to keep it . . . private."

NOTE: Ah, yes. One of the little secrets . . .

[It appears that Mr. Smith has a few secrets, too. Unbeknownst to Mrs. Smith, he called for a separate appointment as well. To review John's file notes, please turn book over and refer to text on page 10.]

JANE

Okay. This feels kind of funny, writing all this down. But here goes.

Here's how I met John.

It was six years ago, and I was staying in the Americana Hotel, in Bogotá, Colombia. I was there to ~~assass~~

I was working on an assignment for my organization. The company I work for. Just something routine.

The place was in total chaos. Politicians were being killed, soldiers raided the buildings on a regular basis, the *policía* ransacked rooms.

Suddenly, one afternoon, the whole town went mad—people flooded the streets, yelling and screaming. I heard a voice shouting in Spanish, *"Somebody shot the Barracuda!"*

The Barracuda—Sancho Varron.

I knew the name well. A local politician who ran the province. Not a good guy. I had . . . heard that he'd been assassinated.

Dark storm clouds threatened overhead, mirroring the mood in the streets, and for both reasons, I decided it might be wise to head indoors. My hair was dark and my Spanish was excellent, but my clothes definitely screamed *"La turista gringa."* Not the best day to stand out in a crowd.

I shoved through the panicked crowd till I reached my hotel. With a glance over my shoulder, I ducked into the doorway.

As my eyes adjusted to the cooler darkness of the lobby, I saw a man sitting at the bar. He was watching the turmoil outside as calmly as if he were watching a parade pass by.

Blond hair, golden tan. Lean but muscular, like a boxer. Stunning good looks.

American business traveler, I guessed. Or maybe a tourist. He was using a dog-eared copy of *Let's Go: South America* as a coaster.

It was the first time I ever laid eyes on John. And I thought at that moment that I would never be able to look away.

A bellboy was telling him the news of the assassination.

"Police are rounding up single tourists!" the young man warned in Spanish.

I never did understand exactly why they did that. Maybe it was something they picked up from American movies. "Are you alone, sir?" he asked John.

I saw him shrug yeah.

Best news I'd heard all day.

He must have felt my stare because he looked up at that moment.

And it took my breath away. He had devastating blue eyes. Eyes a woman could get lost in.

And since I'd completed the day's assignment, I thought I might just like to get lost for a while.

I took a step toward him.

Just then the *policía capitán* stormed into the bar and ruined the party, rounding up suspects and otherwise throwing his weight around. On the slightest whim, he could drag us off to jail, where we might never be seen or heard from again.

My heart pounded as he noticed me. Gave me the once-over, made assumptions, glanced back at John. "You two are together?" the *capitán* asked.

Our eyes met.

And . . . that's all it took, really.

One look—a refuge in the middle of a murderous riot—and John and I were together.

John took my arm as if he'd been waiting for me all afternoon. I gave him a flirtatious hug, then led him toward the stairs.

The *capitán* bought it, looked a little jealous, even, and moved on to terrify other innocent people.

I squeezed John's hand as we continued upstairs.

Looks like we'd dodged another bullet.

JOHN

This is weird.

I'm not sure I can do this.

Okay. Here goes.

Here's how I met Jane.

It was five years ago, and I was in Bogotá, Colombia, to ~~assass~~

Well, I was on an assignment. For my engineering company. I often travel in my work.

I was sitting at the bar in the lobby of the Americana Hotel watching the world erupt into anarchy when a bellboy rushed up to me with news:

"Somebody shot the Barracuda!" he shouted in Spanish.

"Sancho Varron?"

The boy nodded.

No need to tell him it wasn't news to me.

"Police are rounding up single tourists," the boy said, which again was not news. "Are you alone?" he asked.

I was alone. I was always alone. It was the kind of life I led.

Then the *policía capitán* stormed in, no big fucking surprise, backed up by his pack of rats and scaring everybody with his weenie of a gun.

The next thing I knew he was in my face, shouting something.

But suddenly, even though I speak fluent Spanish, I couldn't understand a word he was saying.

Because an absolute vision had just walked in the door, and for a moment, I was oblivious to everything else.

Hair the color of melted chocolate. Gray eyes that could burn a hole in a man's heart. Curves that looked hard and soft at the same time.

I don't know what the hell a woman like that was doing in a place like this. And I didn't care.

I was just glad that out of all the gin joints in the world, she'd walked into mine.

Her smile said she'd noticed me, too.

The *policía capitán* shoved me, demanding my attention.

"What?" I didn't dare tear my eyes away from the vision, in case she tried to disappear.

The *capitán* followed my gaze. "You two are together?" he demanded.

Without a word, I asked her, *Are we?*

Without a word, she answered, *Hell, yeah.*

At least, that was my fantasy translation.

I nodded at the *capitán,* who looked just the tiniest

bit jealous as this goddess gave me a sexy hug and then pulled me toward the stairs.

We continued our charade all the way up to her room, where I assumed the game would end.

But a round of gunfire changed our minds. We ducked inside and slammed the door.

Side by side, leaning against the door, our hearts drumming in our throats, we listened to the shouting, the gunfire, the pounding footsteps. Hoping we'd be among the lucky ones.

I expected my date to scream, or faint, or at least burst into tears.

Instead, she started giggling, like a little girl playing a thrilling game of hide-and-seek.

Jesus! I rolled across her and held my hand over her mouth, inadvertently (yeah, right) pressing the rest of me against the rest of her in the process.

Her eyes widened like I'd made a pass at her.

And hell, maybe I had at that.

Neither of us moved.

I stared down into her clear gray eyes and thought at that moment that I would never be able to look away. I could feel her heart pounding, I could smell the heat of the day on her skin.

Who *was* she? What kind of woman faced danger and laughed?

My kind of a woman.

I knew how I wanted that evening to end.

At sunset, when the day's insanity had quieted down for the night, we escaped the sweltering hotel and ran into the streets.

It had begun to rain by then, people were rushing everywhere. We dashed ahead of them with Spanish newspapers over our heads toward a place I knew down a back alley.

"Varron ran this province for years," I was explaining to her as we ducked beneath an awning.

She nodded. "That's three assassinations this week."

So. She kept up with things.

"Four," I said. "So what brings you to Bogotá?"

"Business." I waited, but she said nothing more. Maybe I should have asked, but hell. I didn't really care why she was there. Just that she was.

"You?" she asked.

"Pleasure."

She seemed to like that answer.

I led her into a basement dive bar, a little place that was popular with the locals.

We'd be safe here. And it was a good place to get drunk without anybody remembering your name.

The dance floor was mobbed with people trying to forget about the world outside; the salsa music was frantic, the dancing hot and furious, and sexy as hell. Not that I ever participated; but I did like to watch.

As I led Jane toward a table in the corner, the danger we'd been in that day seemed to suddenly hit her. "I was right in the street," she said. "I guess I was pretty lucky."

"Trust me," I murmured as I sat and pulled her down beside me. "I'm the lucky one."

I snapped my fingers, and a bottle of tequila slid across our table out of nowhere, followed by all the fixings.

That's what I liked about the place. The service.

And the cheap booze.

I poured out two shots and raised my glass for a toast.

"To dodging bullets . . ." I said.

She smiled and clinked her glass to mine. "To dodging bullets . . ."

My eyes never left hers as we licked the salt from our hands, sucked up the tequila, and bit down into juicy, tangy limes.

It was the single sexiest drink I'd ever had in my life.

Two more and Jane was dragging me onto the grinding, pulsing dance floor. I hollered at her that I didn't dance. But when she threw her arms around me and began to move her hips, she quickly convinced me otherwise.

JANE

*J*ohn said he didn't dance. But that night I thought, if this is how he moves on instinct, he'd be downright dangerous with a few lessons.

It was better than most of the sex I'd had.

I always liked men who knew how to move.

That night I learned the secret of salsa's allure. It was a dance that said, "To hell with today, to hell with tomorrow—tonight we dance."

And so we did, filling our minds with nothing but the moment.

The only thing that finally tore us away from the dance floor was the dress code—clothes. We had to keep them on.

And so, high on tequila, we escaped into the night and tumbled into a cab. There was plenty of room in the backseat, but somehow I found myself curling up on John's lap, where we continued to move to a salsa beat.

When we reached the hotel, our dash up the stairs to my room was no longer a charade.

Later, to escape the sweltering heat inside, we wrapped ourselves in our tangled sheets and climbed out onto the rooftop, where we sat and dangled our feet over the edge. The breeze was heaven on earth, and the clouds had given way to a riotous canopy of stars.

We felt like angels, perched high above the earth on a lofty cloud.

Down below us, a small crowd had gathered on the street to watch an old black-and-white movie projected on a bullet-scarred wall.

One of my favorites—Ginger Rogers and Fred Astaire, twenty feet tall and dancing as if they were made for each other.

And that's how I felt as John pulled me into his arms.

The next morning I woke to sunlight streaming across my face. Delightfully sore from dancing and everything else, I stretched, joyfully aware of being alive. And happier than I'd been in a long time.

Maybe ever.

I rolled over and reached across the bed . . .

And felt nothing but rumpled sheets.

I sighed.

A wonderful night or a beautiful dream?

Either way, it was nice while it lasted. And either way, it had disappeared with the dawn.

Ah, well.

I was used to being alone. I was always alone. It was how I lived my life. By choice.

But it had been nice to think otherwise for a night.

I snuggled back down into my pillow, and tried to recover a wisp of my delicious dream when I heard a key in the lock.

I sat up and pulled the covers around me. Had the *policía* returned?

Then the door opened and there he was. John. As real and as glorious as he'd been in the night.

"Hiya, stranger," I said.

"Hiya back."

He moved toward the bed, his eyes never leaving mine. And he came with gifts.

A steaming cup of coffee and the morning paper.

"I think room service fled," he said. "So I did what I could."

I took a sip of the coffee as he tossed the paper on the bed. "Mmm. *Café con leche.* It's good."

"Better be," John said. "I had to milk the goat myself."

I laughed. "A man who'd risk his life for a cup of coffee. You've gotta love that."

John looked startled, then crossed to the window and pulled back the curtains to stare out into the streets. The glass was shattered from the day before. Black smoke hung in the distance, darkening the sky.

But all I saw was him.

And it was a beautiful morning.

With a sigh I opened up the newspaper, and gasped.

There, tucked in the fold, was a flower. A simple one. The kind of bastard wildflower that shoots up against all odds from the cracks in a battered sidewalk.

It was the most beautiful flower I'd ever seen.

"Anything in the paper?" John asked without turning around.

"Nope," I said with a smile, and slid the flower behind my ear.

Then I picked up the paper again, trying hard not to adore this wonderful man.

Good things, I knew, were as ephemeral as a wildflower in your hair.

The paper was filled with pictures of yesterday's carnage. This place, it was no longer safe. With my work complete, I should have been gone by now.

"You watched me sleep last night," I said casually.

"Did I?" he asked, feigning innocence.

I snuggled back against the pillows and stretched my arms above my head. "What did you see?"

"What did he see . . . ?" John turned and leaned against the windowsill, studying me as if I were some great painting he'd purchased at Sotheby's and just unwrapped in his own home.

I took the moment to study him as well, framed by the window's morning glow. And I came to the conclusion that the man could give Michelangelo's *David* an inferiority complex.

"He saw himself flying home and wishing he'd known her middle name," John said at last. "And her?"

His answer surprised me. I was touched, and falling quickly under his spell.

It was a lovely feeling, a part of me thought.

And far too dangerous, countered another.

Many words sprang to my lips. I was very good at games of the heart, so I knew to keep things light, flirtatious.

"She saw herself walking through Chinatown," I said, "and wondering how he felt about jazz." A clever, sexy line, I decided.

"And he," John vollied, "thought that maybe there is something more sublime than the perfect putt on the eighteenth green on a sunny Sunday morning."

Be still, my heart, my grin answered, as I drew the covers up to my chin. "And she thought how much he'd love her lemon cake," I said playfully.

Suddenly he was towering over me, and the playfulness in his voice was replaced by an intensity that took my breath away. "He suspected that last night would be the night by which all other nights were measured."

His eyes dared me to step out from behind the security of coy phrases. And so, in spite of being scared, I answered honestly. "And she agreed."

John leaned down, his face inches from mine, his blue eyes guarded.

So. We were both afraid. And with that knowledge, a giddiness began to bubble up in my heart.

"What happens next?" he whispered.

"Everything," I said.

He growled like a starving tiger as we fell into each other's arms, into a kiss that felt as if it would never end.

JOHN

aaand step right up, ladies and gentlemen!"

Jane and I were strolling through the San Gennaro street festival, one of New York City's oldest and biggest street fairs, held in Manhattan's Little Italy.

Yeah, that's right.

We'd traded streets—one filled with murder and mayhem for one overflowing with laughter, music, and celebration.

We'd left Bogotá and flown home. And, well, let's just say we'd stayed in touch. *Very much* in touch.

No more bullets to dodge. Instead, Jane and I dodged the crowds as we shared pink cotton candy and browsed the stalls offering food, crafts, games, and other things to spend money on.

"Come on, little lady, don't be afraid!"

The ancient barker working the shooting gallery had no idea who he was talking to. I didn't think my Jane was afraid of anything.

It didn't escape my notice that I was already thinking of her as mine.

Jane slowed down and seemed attracted to the toy guns.

"Want to try your luck?" I suggested.

Her killer lips curled into a smile, considering. "Why not?"

As I paid the man, Jane selected a gun. It looked a little awkward in her hands, but I resisted the urge to correct her hold. It was just for fun, after all.

She aimed, fired—*blam!* The gun had quite a kickback. Jane stumbled a little and missed.

I urged her to try again.

The next time she almost blinded the barker!

Poor guy. I tried not to laugh as she shrugged and handed the gun to me.

I took the weapon in my hands, testing the weight, rolled my neck to loosen up. Then took aim.

What is it about carnivals, girls, and guns that just makes you want to show off?

I fired—and bull's-eyed the target.

Jane gasped, and looked very impressed.

I shrugged. "Beginner's luck, I guess."

Hell, I didn't want to make her feel bad. So I decided not to try so hard with my next shot. I had other reasons, too, for not wanting to show off in public just how good I was with a gun.

So I took a few more shots, this time dipping down, missing a couple for good measure.

All in all, not bad for your average Joe. Even trying to miss, I won a small stuffed bear. Proud of myself, I turned to walk away and offer the prize to my girl.

But Jane stopped me. "Um, may I have another go?"

Ah, I thought. *Competitive, are we?* I liked that in a woman.

This time she held the gun like a pro, raised it to her eye, and fired off five rounds in a row.

Blam! Blam! Blam! Blam! Blam!

I nearly dropped my bear.

Five shots. Five perfect bull's-eyes.

"Beginner's luck, I guess," she said as she walked off with her prize: a *life-size* stuffed bear.

I guess I must have looked stunned. With a laugh, she slipped the scarf from around her bear's neck and whipped it around mine.

She had me where she wanted me. She could have ended my life with a hard twist.

But instead she pulled me close and ended my life as I knew it . . . with a killer kiss.

Goddamn. She was the girl of my dreams.

JANE

Okay, so now I was scared.

It had been six weeks since John and I met in Bogotá. Six weeks!

And now he wanted to take me out someplace really special for dinner. Dress up, he said.

So, you might ask, what was I scared of?

The six-weeks part.

I hadn't been in a relationship that lasted longer than six weeks since I took piano lessons in second grade.

And that only lasted for seven.

Good things never lasted. And this thing between John and me? It was good. Very, very good.

So of course it had to end. And soon.

Hell, for all I knew, this could be our last night together.

So I dressed up as if I had something to celebrate. Even though I might only be toasting adieu.

We could have walked, but John suggested we take a taxi, since I was wearing heels.

I secretly think taking cabs reminded him of our first night in Bogotá.

All too soon we arrived at the River Café. I suggested we drink tequila for old time's sake, but John ordered champagne.

"Champagne is for celebrating," he said.

I smiled, blinking away the sudden moisture in my eyes.

We drank champagne, we watched the river, but mostly we stared at each other. We'd ordered food, but it sat there between us, untouched. I was hungry, but only for him.

I think there was music; I think people danced.

But just as in Bogotá, we seemed oblivious to everything, as if our lives were lived at the eye of a hurricane while the rest of the world stormed around us.

I wondered wildly if there was some way to make this night last forever. Maybe we could lasso the moon and ride it forever through the stars, so the dream would never end.

Not the kind of thoughts I usually entertained. But then, that's what being with John did to me.

That's when John's hand moved to his pocket. I thought it was for a pen, at first. Or a cigarette?

But instead he pulled out a small box. Light blue, the shade that Tiffany's is known for.

I couldn't make sense of what I was seeing.

John didn't say a word. He just opened the box.

And then the whole world sparkled as he slid a ring on my left hand.

John had given me the stars—and a night that would last forever.

JOHN

STOP!" my best friend and coworker Eddie exclaimed. The next day I was working out in my regular boxing gym with a trainer. I'd been telling Eddie about Jane, and he did not like what he was hearing.

"You're *what*?"

"I'm in love," I said.

Eddie looked at me as if I'd taken too many blows to the head. "You've know her, what, six weeks?"

But how could I explain to Eddie? He changed women more often than he changed his socks. "This girl, Eddie—she's . . . wild. She's strong, and she's *competitive*. I don't know how to describe it. I feel like . . ."

Pow! I slammed into the bag.

JANE

You don't think this is happening a *little* fast?"

The next day I was climbing with my best friend and coworker Jasmine.

I always found this sport to be a great way to work out, but today I found it especially exhilarating and had to struggle not to leave Jasmine far behind.

But she wasn't talking about my climbing speed. She was talking about my relationship with John.

"You know me," I said, glancing back down. "I don't do anything rashly—watch your foothold."

She did. "So what does he do?"

"Construction. He's a big-league contractor."

"Great," Jasmine said sarcastically. "So he lays cement."

I laughed. "That's not all."

JOHN

She's in computers," I told Eddie. "A server goes down in Wall Street, she's in there anytime day or night. She's like Batman for computers. Or something."

JANE

and the sex . . . ?" Jasmine asked.

JOHN

Wham! I let loose with a thundering punch, knocking my sparring partner off his feet.

Eddie whistled. "That good, huh?"

JANE

I had reached the top of the cliff, and the view was magnificent. I'd always been athletic—my job required me to stay in shape. But I had never felt more energetic.

I suspected it had something to do with my workouts with John.

But Jasmine was still a ways behind me, and still skeptical. Sex is sex, was her attitude. Why complicate it with things like relationships?

"You don't worry that, you know, your *work* schedule might foul things up?" she asked.

"Use the crag on your left," I suggested. And yes, I'd thought of that. There would be some...complications, sometimes. But I was sure it was nothing I couldn't work out. "He travels a lot, like me," I explained. "So it's not a problem—"

I pulled her up beside me. And ignored her worried frown.

JOHN

—and, what, am I supposed to sacrifice any personal life I have for my job?" I asked Eddie.

I kept working with my trainer. My endurance was better than ever.

I smiled. You might think Jane and I would wear each other out. That's how the old sports advice went. But instead it was having just the opposite effect. I had more energy and drive than ever.

Jab, cross, duck . . . jab, cross, duck . . . I felt like I could go on like this for hours.

But Eddie was not convinced. To him sex was just something that kept breakfast, lunch, and dinner from being one continuous meal.

"I give this six months, tops," he said. "No way it lasts longer than that."

"Eddie," I confessed. "I asked her to marry me."

"What?!"

"I'm getting married."

Whack! Eddie was so startled by my news, he walked right into my trainer's glove.

He went down, hard.

He was never going to forgive me for the news.

JANE

*J*ohn and I got married in the city clerk's office. We couldn't wait any longer. Jasmine was my maid of honor, and John's friend Eddie stood up for him as best man.

They both looked mad as hell.

But we barely noticed. When John slipped the ring on my finger, our hands shook. It was the first time in my life anyone had promised me anything.

"–if any party should feel opposed to this union," the clerk said, "let them speak now or forever hold their peace."

I saw Jasmine biting her tongue, and I made a face at her to stop.

I'd show her.

JOHN

I was afraid Eddie would burst when the clerk said that bit about speaking now or forever holding your peace. It took everything he had to restrain himself.

He still thought I was nuts. But I'd told him he could only stand up as my best man at the wedding if he promised not to say a word.

And I warned him I'd punch him out if he dared.

So we made it through the ceremony.

My hands shook as I slipped the ring on Jane's finger, but she just glowed.

And then the clerk said, "I now pronounce you husband and wife. Mr. and Mrs. Smith."

Mr. and Mrs. Smith. I liked the way that sounded.

And when he said, "You may kiss the bride," well . . .

We kissed until the Korean couple waiting to go next complained.

JANE

The last assignment Dr. Wexler gave me wasn't all that painful, so I'm ready to give this one a try, too. The good doctor wants me to write about my life *now,* so here goes . . .

~~I am~~

~~John and I are~~

~~John is~~

Okay, this is harder than I thought.

Maybe I'll just write about last night.

I was making dinner, like most nights.

Ping! The timer chimed and I peeked inside the oven. Everything looked perfect.

But, of course, it wasn't.

Six years is a long time. Things change.

People change.

My perfect life . . . isn't really perfect.

So I just keep trying to make it that way.

The house, the yard, the food. I throw myself into everything with the same ambition and competitiveness that drives my work.

Like dinner. I can dance around this kitchen, chopping vegetables and tossing pans like I was Jackie Chan. I can plan, organize, and prepare a dinner for fifty that would put the White House to shame.

And I do it every night for two.

Even after a long hard day at work, like last night. I cooked a savory meal, set the table, and chilled the wine so everything would be absolutely perfect.

Even though it never was.

But what else could I do? I had to keep trying.

I heard a car in the driveway, and looked up as headlights splashed through the window. *Why do I always tense up these days the moment John arrives?* I wondered.

Remember who you are, I reminded myself. *You're smart, you're strong. You can do anything.*

I snatched up my knife and twirled it over my fingers before slamming it into its block.

Yeah, anything but save my own marriage.

JOHN

Okay. It was hard enough writing about the past. About Bogotá. That was one thing.

But now Doc Wexler wants me to write about what's going on today—in our marriage.

I told him—he's a guy, he should know—we don't do this kind of stuff very easily.

"That's the point," he said. He thinks there's a lot of stuff bothering me. Like shit deep down inside. Stuff that I avoid thinking about. Stuff I never deal with. And that sometimes the only way to address it is to get it all out in a journal.

"Hey, the punching bag usually works for me," I joked.

Dr. Wexler didn't laugh.

So here I am.

◎ ๓ ๓ ◎ ๓

Okay. I couldn't figure out how to start. So I called Dr. Wexler to say that it wasn't working but thanks anyway. I was about to hang up and forget the whole thing, but he stopped me.

He's a persistent bastard, you know. He just said, "Relax, John. Remember this is not homework." Then he reminded me that there are no right or wrong answers here.

He suggested that I start by writing about last night. "Just write down what you remember," he said. "The rest will come."

I reluctantly said okay, I'd give it a whirl.

So here I go.

Last night.

I pulled into the driveway and eased the sedan into the garage.

For a moment I just sat there, listening to the engine hum as I got my act together. It had been a long day, and the world I'd been in was light-years away from the one waiting for me in that house.

Five years was a long time.

Things changed. People changed.

Or maybe . . . maybe everything just faded. Like a newspaper lying in the sun.

Might as well go in, I thought finally. Jane's hearing rivals Superman's, so I felt sure she knew I was home. If I sat here too long, she'd come flying out to see what was wrong.

I unbuckled my seat belt and—

Damn! Where was my ring? I'd almost forgotten to put it back on. I searched my pockets and found it in my coat, then slipped it back on my left ring finger.

I glanced at myself in the rearview mirror. *Pay attention, man.*

Hell, what was that? A smudge of red on my collar.

Shit, that'd send Jane through the roof. I rubbed it, but no way was it coming out. So I managed to tuck my collar in a bit, hiding the stain.

Then I hurried into the house.

Once inside, I tossed my keys into a bowl in the foyer. Wondering, certainly not for the first time, why I felt so tense every time I walked in the front door.

Jane appeared out of nowhere. "Perfect timing," she said with a smile. She looked at me expectantly.

Oh, yeah. The butter. Thank God I didn't forget. I'd never hear the end of it. With a flourish I pulled the carton from my coat pocket. "You ask for butter? I bring you butter."

"Good day?" she asked as she took it.

I shrugged. "Same old same old. You?"

She mirrored my shrug. Hesitated.

I leaned down to deliver the obligatory kiss.

Bad move. I saw her frown as she pulled away. Which meant she obviously noticed the smell of alcohol on my breath.

"I stopped off for one with Eddie," I said casually.

Jane nodded, not hiding her displeasure very well.

And I'm sure I didn't hide mine well, either. She was always on my case about the drinking.

But now there was something more. She was staring at the butter like it was a two-headed snake. "This is salted," she complained.

She held up the carton so I could see it; yep, it said SALTED right there on the front. I blinked. "Does it come any other way?"

"*Un*-salted," she said. Adding under her breath, "Like I asked for."

I groaned inwardly. Why did she keep giving me

these ridiculous errands to do when she was never satisfied with how I did them? It was like an ice princess sending the poor beleaguered knight out on some quest that he could never fulfill. I tried to apologize, but she just waved it away.

"It's all right. I'll just, uh, work around it."

Hey, if that's your toughest lump of the day . . .

Fortunately she tried to change the subject. "I got new curtains for the living room," she said cheerfully.

"You did?"

"I did."

She led me into the already perfectly decorated living room to show me the new green curtains that we didn't need, draped over the sofa. They were huge; the color overwhelmed everything else in sight.

"There was a tug-of-war over the material when I found it," she said. "This tea sandwich of a man got his hands on it, too, but I won."

"Of course you did." *She always does.*

"I figured with the boldness of the solid, we should consider maybe finding a checkered cover for the couch," she went on, "something not too busy, not a floral obviously, and definitely lighter than the curtains, which means we should get a darker Persian for the floor."

My eyes were glazing over, and I felt a headache coming on. So we were getting curtains that we didn't need, which meant we would have to change the couch covers to match the curtains, and then the rug to match the new couch covers that we wouldn't have had to buy if we didn't get new curtains to begin with.

"Or here's a thought," I said. "We could just stick with the old curtains."

She looked up and frowned. Sure took her long enough to realize she was having a conversation with herself about something that irritated the hell out of me.

"What? We talked about this. Don't you remember?"

"Yeah," I said. "Because we decided to wait."

I sighed at the miserable look on her face.

My happy little homecoming was over.

Jane smoothed the already smoothed-out curtains. "If you don't like them, I can take them back—"

"I *don't* like them—"

"Well, *get used to them!*"

The silence was staggering. How the hell had we gotten to this point again? All hope of a pleasant evening was gone, which was exactly where *I* wanted to be.

"I think I'll go water—"

"I should work on the—"

Mercifully, we allowed each other to escape.

Outside, I turned on the hose and sprayed the flowers along the driveway. Not that they needed it. But *I* needed it. I liked the sound of water. It was soothing. Made me think of rivers, flowing away downstream.

I spotted a basketball lying among the tulips. Was it my old one, or had some kid left it behind?

Man, it had been ages since I shot hoops. On a whim, I scooped up the ball and took a shot at the basket mounted on the garage.

Then I turned around, picked up the hose, and went back to watering.

Thirty feet behind me, I heard the ball sing through the hoop.

I could sink a shot without even looking.

But this marriage . . . it was getting harder and harder to even try.

JANE

He didn't care about the curtains. He never even thought about the house. I'm not sure he cared about *anything* in the house. Including me. So why did he make such a fuss? Why did he have to ruin something that mattered so much to me?

He never seemed to care that things were always the same. What was wrong with a little change now and then? Change is good. Sometimes I get so bored staring at the same things over and over, I think I'm going nuts. Sometimes, I think, if I didn't have my job to escape to every day . . .

Forget about it, I told myself. *Just fix the curtains. They'll look great, he'll see. It'll be a nice change.*

I stood on a chair and snapped the panel over the rod. But the chair was too low. I still needed to reach higher to fully straighten out the fabric. So I stood with one foot on the arm of the chair, the other foot on the top corner, and then I stretched until the curtain hung just right.

Thanks to my job and climbing workouts, I could balance like a mountain goat on the top of a pin.

Perfect.

But then I heard John come in. I jumped down instantly.

He looked up from the mail just as I stepped off the chair, missing my skilled acrobatics by seconds.

I smiled at him. "What do you think?"

He looked at the curtains, then back at me. The best he could offer was a weak smile.

We sleepwalked through the meal, as usual. John was polite as always, saying his lines, complimenting the food.

I could have been *anybody,* said *anything,* and none of it would have mattered. Sometimes I felt like a ghost.

Invisible.

Most nights I felt like jumping up and shouting, *Look at me! I'm alive! Ask me something. Yell at me. Anything but this!* Sometimes I want to shout, *Let me tell you what I* really *did today. You wouldn't believe it!*

Instead, I just pick up my knife and slice off another piece of meat.

JOHN

She makes such a big deal out of dinner every single night. I mean, I told her a long time ago, Jane, you don't have to do this. I didn't marry you just so you could cook for me.

I mean, can't we just have a frozen pizza or some microwave nachos sometimes?

But no. It has to be this perfect dinner every time, like something out of a magazine. I don't know, maybe that's what it was like in her house growing up.

So that night we sat at opposite ends of our huge table in the dining room. Candles flickering and all. But everything I did seemed to irritate her.

I drank my wine and refilled the glass. That seemed to bug her. Guess she thought I was drinking too much again.

Then I complimented her on the food. I mean, it looked beautiful—almost too beautiful to eat. And I asked her, "You do something new with it?"

"I added peas," she said.

"Ah. Peas," I said. I scooped up a huge mouthful. "Mmm. It's good."

What'd I say? She looked like she was ready to blow.

So I gave up and ate in silence for a while. And then I asked her to pass the salt.

Well, you wouldn't think passing the salt would be such a big issue. But she stages these little battles of will, which she's got to win at all cost.

"Could you pass the salt, please?" I asked.

For some reason, she looked annoyed. "It's in the middle of the table."

I looked. And well, to tell you the truth, it looked like it was a little closer to her end of the table than mine. Not that it really mattered. But *she* was the one who made it into a contest. "Is that the middle?" I snapped.

"It's between you and me," she said.

Damn. So I screeched back my chair, got up, walked to the middle of the table—her side of the middle—and grabbed the salt.

You should have seen the smile of victory on her face.

Till I sat back down—and *drowned* her precious dinner in salt.

Jane swallowed her smile.

Let me tell you, I had a hard time swallowing my dinner, too, with all that salt.

But it was worth it. This time, I'd won.

I wasn't sure *what* I'd won, exactly. But . . . I'd won.

JANE

Later that night, after managing to avoid each other all evening in our large perfect home, we found ourselves in our bedroom. Bedtime usually comes when there's no way to put it off any longer.

Sometimes I go to sleep early while John stays up working

in his office or the den. Or when he's puttering around out back in his toolshed.

Sometimes I stay up late, finding little things to do in the kitchen. Or I watch an old black-and-white movie on TV. Sometimes I even fall asleep on the couch. Accidentally, of course. John usually leaves me there, and the next morning says he didn't want to wake me.

But some nights I think, if we could just go to bed together, and talk . . . really talk . . .

But we never do.

Tonight I was already in bed, reading a novel, when John came in, dressed in his pajamas, and slid in beside me. He busied himself with his alarm clock, his covers, his pillow.

I laid my book down. A sign that I . . . could be interrupted. To talk. Or whatever.

But of course, he didn't look at me. He was rarely interested in interruptions anymore.

"Well," he said to the foot of the bed. "I'm bushed."

I shut my heart against the rebuff. It got easier every time.

"Me, too," I said quickly. "Busy day tomorrow."

"Good night, sweetie," John said. He paused a moment, and I waited hopefully.

Then all he said was, "Love you."

I swallowed. "Love you, too," I echoed.

When did we drop the *I*? I wondered. When did *I love you* turn into the abbreviation *Love you*?

It really didn't mean the same.

"How're ya doing?"

"Have a nice day."

"Love you."

Meaningless expressions that people said without thinking.

I sighed and turned off my bedside lamp. John turned off his. We settled down in the darkness.

I closed my eyes and could almost believe I was all alone.

Which, I sometimes thought, might just be easier than this.

JOHN

Well, you can imagine what it was like in the bedroom that night.

Jane was already tucked in, reading. I waited as long as I could before hitting the sack, hoping maybe she'd fall asleep.

But I was tired, dog tired, and finally I just couldn't put it off any longer.

I changed into my pajamas in the bathroom, then climbed into bed.

She put down her book. Looked at me expectantly.

But what the hell did she think, really? I mean, to be honest . . . there hadn't been a whole lot going on in that room except sleeping for . . . well, for a long time. And after the evening we'd had . . .

"Well, I'm bushed," I said, fussing with my covers. Trying to yawn.

She just looked away. "Yeah, me, too. Busy day tomorrow."

She sounded so hurt, I felt like a heel. But I didn't know what in the hell I could do about it. I figured the best thing I could do was just go to sleep, and put us both out of our misery.

"Good night, sweetie," I said, forcing the affection. "Love you."

"Love you, too," she said. Automatically. Like she always does. She never says it first anymore. But if I say it first, she says it back.

"How are you?"

"Fine, and you?"

"Love you."

"Love you, too."

It was a relief when we just turned out the lights.

I mean, maybe I could have said something. Or touched her hand. Offered a small gesture that would have made a difference.

Maybe . . .

But I was tired.

Tired of trying, too.

I can't make myself feel something I don't.

I mean, really, what did she expect?

JANE

a few nights later John and I were doing the dishes together.

A chore, a ritual. We didn't talk.

John scrubbed the plates under running water, and I put them in the dishwasher. That's how we always did it.

What if we just got *totally* crazy and switched places? I could scrape and rinse—and he could load?!

I guess our marriage couldn't stand the excitement.

His mind was elsewhere, as usual. Thinking about something or someone else. Work, I guess. I could have whacked him over the head with one of the plates, I thought, and he still wouldn't notice me.

Then, absentmindedly, he handed me a plate that was still caked with food.

I mean, I *told* myself, *Jane, don't make an issue out of it. Just put it in the dishwasher.*

But really, why not do things right? I knew the plate would come out still dirty, and worse, caked with food baked on by the heat of the drying cycle. So I squeezed past him to lean over the sink and scraped the food into the garbage disposal.

Well, he didn't say a word. Just made this face he makes. Pursed his lips, like some old sourpuss. You would have thought I'd insulted his tie.

Luckily the phone rang.

My eyes shot to the phone on the wall. So did John's.

Line two was lit up. My line.

"Office," I said, and quickly snapped up the receiver. "Just be a sec." I dashed out of the kitchen, and up the stairs.

Leaving John to do whatever the hell he wanted to with the goddamn dishes.

JOHN

I watched Jane go. Ducking her head, covering up the receiver as she spoke into the phone.

She sure got a lot of calls from the office.

I stared at the dirty plate in my hands as I listened to her pounding up the stairs, to our bedroom. Where she couldn't be heard.

I listened anyway.

The faucet dripped in the sink.

Nothing.

Then I took that dirty plate and stuck it straight into the goddamn dishwasher. *Without* scrubbing it clean first.

Just a tiny act of rebellion.

Hey, a guy had to do something every now and then to protect his manhood.

Suddenly I heard a strange scraping noise upstairs, over my head. Like furniture being dragged across the floor. Or a body.

My eyes narrowed. Now what?

Not that I cared. But . . . maybe Jane needed some help.

Casually, quietly, I stole up the stairs toward our bedroom. As I moved down the hallway, I could see our door was open a little. Just enough for me to peek inside.

Jane, her back to me, had just slipped on her coat. Still talking quietly into the phone, I heard her say, "Mmm-hmm . . . uh-huh . . . Penthouse suite. Be there in forty-five."

Penthouse suite, huh?

She hung up, and I took a step back. But the floor creaked, just the tiniest bit.

She spun around and saw me, standing in the doorway. "Jesus, honey, you almost gave me a heart attack."

"Sorry," I said with a casual shrug. "Just wanted to make sure everything was all right."

She rolled her eyes and swung her arm toward the phone. "Some clown just crashed a server at a law firm downtown, and ended the world as they know it." Her movements seemed exaggerated, her voice a little too loud. She shrugged apologetically. "Gotta go to the city."

"We promised the Colemans," I reminded her.

She stiffened, and checked her watch. "I'll be back by nine. In and out. Just a quickie," she added.

I kinda wished she hadn't used that word.

She smiled. I smiled. A formality, really. I guess we were both half relieved to be free of each other's company for a few hours.

I waited till I heard the front door slam, then traced her path down the stairs.

I stood at the front window and watched her back out of the driveway. Not for the first time, I wondered where she was really going. What she'd be doing. Who she'd be doing it with.

Maybe she wondered the same things when I went out.

When did we stop asking?

Hell, when did we stop really caring?

Her headlights hit me like a searchlight, then she was gone.

A clock ticked on the mantel.

Suddenly our perfect house seemed too big, too empty.

Lucky for me, I had a little errand to run myself.

Half an hour later I was riding across the Queensboro Bridge with my hired chauffeur—a guy named Yousef. I couldn't quite decide if Yousef was happy or pissed to be driving me and his cab into the city. Probably a little of both. Brother, I know the feeling. His driving sucked.

I was still wearing my suit, but I loosened my tie. Easier for the booze to go down that way.

And boy, could I use a drink. Yousef's cab was a little short on amenities—like a window that worked and a well-stocked limo bar. But no matter, since I always traveled with my own personal wet bar: a silver hip flask. Top-of-the-line Scotch. What else do you need to know? I pulled the flask from my pocket and twisted off the cap.

I held it out a moment as we bounced over something in the road, then found my eyes tracing the engraving. How long had it been since I'd actually read those words?

To dodging bullets. Love, Jane.

Yeah. Here's to you, too, babe.

I took a long drink.

Yousef looked like he could use a shot himself as we pulled up in front of the address I'd given him. The street was dark, ominously quiet. Trash skittered like rats along the sidewalks. Or maybe it *was* just rats.

I paid the cabbie, tipping him enough to go get so fucking drunk, he'd forget he ever saw me. As soon as I stepped out on the street, he tore off like the devil was after him, and I was alone.

I did a slow three-sixty, then headed down some dank stairs that led to a blacked-out door. I jabbed a buzzer, and after a moment, the door clicked open.

I stepped inside and looked around.

Jeez. Maybe Yousef had it right. This place was definitely the last stop before hell.

A bare bulb hung over the cash register, revealing some strung-out hookers barely hanging on to the bar. Darkness spared me from whatever else was going on in the stinking room.

I sat down on a stool that seemed in danger of plunging through the rotting wood floor. Found my balance. Waited for the bartender to acknowledge me.

At last he glared at me like he'd just heard I'd screwed his mother. *"Yeah?"*

"What kind of beer can I get?" I asked.

"Guinness . . ."

I waited, but he didn't say anything else. Guess that narrowed down the choices.

"I'll have a Red Label and soda," I said instead. "Go stingy on the soda."

While he poured my drink I leaned on the bar and studied the decor. Now that my eyes had grown used to the darkness, I could see that the shadows cloaked various felonies in progress: drugs, gambling, cash being exchanged for lumpy bags. A few other things in the corners I didn't want to think about.

Beyond that, a partly drawn curtain led to a hall-way and further secret hiding places.

The bartender slammed my drink on the bar. Maybe he thought I was looking a little too nosy. So I turned back around and stared down into my drink. It was black.

Sure didn't look like Red Label and soda.

But the bartender's look told me he didn't take criticism well, so, what the hell—booze was booze—I sucked it down.

Whoa! That would do the trick. "Hit me again, will ya?" I said, beginning to slur my words a little. He gave me a hard look, so I decided not to linger. "Where's the john around here?" I complained, and he nodded toward the curtain in the rear.

As soon as he served me my fresh drink—and I'm us-ing the words *served* and *fresh* loosely here—I headed through the curtains and staggered down the hallway till I found two doors. One was marked: PISSER. The other read: KEEP THE FUCK OUT.

High-class place, this joint.

You gotta know this about me. All my life I've had major issues with "Keep Out" signs. Something about them piss me off. Just can't ignore them. So I chose the one less traveled by, and stumbled through the door.

"What the fuck!" somebody shouted.

I'd barged in on a poker game. Very private. Very backroom. Three extremely untrustworthy-looking char-acters and one all-around badass motherfucker stared at me in disbelief.

"What is this shit?" somebody shouted.

"Sorry," I slurred. "Was looking for the can." I started to leave, then, swaying a little, turned back. "You guys playing poker?"

"Private game," one guy said. "Get the fuck out."

"You've got an empty chair," I pointed out.

Another guy twisted in his seat and glared at me. "What part of 'fuck the fuck off' didn't you understand?"

"You sure?" Swaying, I tried to get my hand in my pocket. "I got plenty of . . ."

The big mother was on his feet with a semiautomatic pointed at my forehead before I could finish my sentence.

I froze. "Hey, It's just my roll." Slowly I pulled my hand from my pocket and showed him a thick wad of bills.

A few whispered words passed between them. Nothing I could catch, but I heard someone call the badass guy Curtis. I got the feeling he was top dog.

I could see Curtis thinking: *Shit-faced rich boy with a pocket full of dead presidents needing to make a deposit.* Who could have a problem with that?

Almost in. "I just thought, you got an empty chair—"

"That's Lucky's chair," Curtis snapped.

Just what I wanted to hear. "When is Lucky getting here?"

He grunted. "Whenever Lucky *wants* to get here."

"Well, let me play till he shows," I said. "C'mon, you know I got money."

The guys at the table traded looks, looks they thought I couldn't read: *Why not have a little fun while we wait for Lucky?*

Curtis kicked the empty chair out from the table. Smiling like a dope, I sank into Lucky's chair.

JANE

*J*switched vehicles in my usual discreet manner once I got into the city. "Another day, another dollar," I muttered to myself as I hopped into the backseat of the Yellow Cab that would whisk me downtown to my assignment.

Midnight runs were nothing unusual in my line of work. And what I did for a living definitely paid better than minimum wage.

God! If John only knew what I did when I escaped our suffocating life in the middle of the night.

What would he think?

Would he even care?

I shivered and gazed out at the city flying past. The crowds, the bright lights filling the night sky, always reminded me of a beach carnival someone took me to when I was little—someone whose face I can no longer quite remember. Soaring rides, sideshow freaks—I squealed in delighted terror at it all, tethered to safety by a strong hand that swung me high in the air, but never let me go.

And then, one day, did.

Damn.

Focus, I told myself. *You've got a job to do.*

I rolled down the window to let the fresh air whisk away old heartaches. I chose a building up ahead and began to count the floors, a little game I often played while riding taxis. First I estimated the number of floors, how many apartments on each floor, how many people in each apartment. Then I tried to calculate how many people might be living in the whole building.

How many people were at that very moment flushing the toilet? Eating Chinese takeout? Making love?

How many ordinary people? How many secrets?

At last the driver pulled over to the curb. I stared up through the window at my destination: the very elegant, the very tasteful, the very expensive Hudson Hotel. Booked solid, every night.

Who were all these people? I wondered. And what in the world did they all do to earn enough money to stay here, instead of the Motel 6 off the New Jersey Turnpike?

Upstairs, on one of those golden floors, one of those lucky guests was waiting for me. Was perhaps even salivating with anticipation of my arrival.

And it was my job to give him the night of his life.

So to speak.

And I knew exactly what he did to be able to afford the place.

I overpaid the driver, whispered in his ear that he'd never seen me, then grabbed my doctor's bag and stepped out, careful not to dirty my high-heeled black boots in the gutter.

As I walked toward the hotel, my coat fell open, and the doorman nearly dropped to his knees.

Good. That was exactly the effect I was hoping my client would have to the all-black-leather outfit I'd chosen.

Men were always easier to handle when they were on their knees.

I moved like a panther through the hotel lobby, trying not to attract attention, but the men, always hunting, kept their sights trained on my carcass till I reached the elevator.

Once inside, I caressed the long list of numbers, then pressed PENTHOUSE. Nothing but the best for this man.

And that included me.

Even so, I was going to be a helluva lot more than he'd bargained for.

I had been doing this for years, long before I met my husband. Even after we married, I continued my . . . *private* career.

I was experienced. Well trained. A true professional. And I prided myself on being the best woman in the business.

Ding! The elevator stopped at the top floor. The doors hissed open.

Showtime, I thought, and felt a rush—that surge of adrenaline that I always got just before I went to work.

How many secretaries or computer programmers could say *that*?

At the double doors to the penthouse suite, I was greeted by a bodyguard the size and shape of a Sub-Zero refrigerator. Deluxe model.

"You Carlotta?" he grunted.

I just smiled and stepped inside.

As he locked the door behind me, I quickly surveyed the room—doors, windows, floor plan. In the main living area, four more bodyguards—each one uglier than the next—huddled around the TV watching the Game Show Network.

I smiled. A couple of Einsteins. *Perfect.*

"What's in the bag?" Sub-Zero demanded.

I didn't answer, but simply opened it for his inspection. One by one he pulled out my tools of the trade: A long wicked whip. A set of bondage cuffs. A cat-o'-nine-tails.

The stuff didn't even faze him.

Guess his boss had done this kind of thing before.

Sub stuffed the items back into the bag and shoved the bag into my arms. "We have a plane in an hour," he warned.

I winked. "I'm the fastest gun in the West."

With a bored grunt, he motioned to a hallway off the living room, then turned back to the TV.

The goons were trying to guess a clip from an old movie, and they didn't have a clue. *In more ways than one.*

But the movie was easy. Black-and-white, Cary Grant. Charming little flick about a dead body.

It was one of my favorites.

"*Arsenic and Old Lace,*" I tossed over my shoulder as I headed down the hall.

They exclaimed various expletives when the game-show host confirmed that I was right.

Guys like these never expected a woman to have a brain in her head. They thought we were only good for one thing.

Their mistake. Lucky for me, though. It made my job that much easier when they underestimated me.

And now it was time to do it. On full alert, I slipped into the bedroom and closed the door.

I was greeted by sounds of gargling and spitting: my host "freshening up" in the adjoining bathroom.

Good. That gave me a few minutes to scope out my setup.

Huge bed with zebra-print linens. (Yuck.)

French windows that led to a generous rooftop balcony. (Excellent.)

I set my bag on the bed and opened it, then paused.

I could smell my client sneaking up behind me.

I turned around and gave him my sexiest smile.

The groan he let out was almost a bark. He reminded me of a German shepherd about to pounce on a plate of raw steak.

Marco Racin. A slick, sleazy Euro. Fifty-something. Tubby. *Tsk, Tsk, Marco. How you've let yourself go,* I thought.

But my face said, *Come here, you sexy hunk! I'm paid for and I'm all yours!*

He slowly walked around me, licking his lips as he admired the merchandise. Unaffected, I stood and let him look, hoping he'd work himself into a state that would make him putty in my hands. After a few moments, I moved to the door and locked it. Then turned around.

He was pawing through the bag I'd left on the bed.

"See anything you like?" I purred. With a snap of a clasp, my overcoat fell to the floor, revealing my evening wear: black dominatrix gear.

"Much," he slobbered.

Then he swept me into his sweaty arms and whispered in my ear—something I'd just as soon not write down here.

"They still put you in jail for that, baby," I murmured.

"Not in my country," he growled.

Okay. He was ready. Time to make my move.

I cracked my knuckles, shoved him down on the bed, and reached for the bag.

JOHN

Shit!" I threw my cards on the table.

My new buddy Mickey grinned and raked in the pot.

"I was so close!" I whined.

The rest of the guys just laughed and winked at one another, like I couldn't see everything they did.

Changing dealers didn't help my game much, and the results were pretty much the same. "Damn!" I complained when my other new best friend, P.J., won the next hand. "That was . . . Damn!"

My poker buddies had been reluctant to let me play at first. But it was amazing: The longer I played, the friendlier they got.

After three losing hands, I started to show signs of confusion and doubt, but they encouraged me to "keep trying." What a couple of pals, eh?

When Curtis upped the ante in the next game, I blurted out, "Call!" then "No—fold!" then "No! Call!" until P.J. reminded me I was playing out of turn. And then I lost again.

"Shit!" I cried, when P.J. bluffed me into folding three nines to beat me with a pair of deuces. "I had that!"

P.J. pulled his winnings—most of it my money—into his arms, then turned to me with a look of pity. "Homes, you got fourteen different tells," he said. "Motherfucker, you are William Tell."

Mickey leaned back in his chair and sang the melody to the famous overture, and everybody laughed.

I was impressed; they'd obviously picked up quite a lot of culture from the classical-music sound tracks used in the cartoons they watched.

Curtis's turn to deal. By now I was so down, I was almost under the table—both from my card playing and my drinking. Did they see the panic in my eyes? I made a vague glance in Curtis's direction.

"Don't be stealing no look, Casper," he warned. He shifted in his chair so I could see the gun tucked in his pants—the same semiautomatic I'd gotten up close and personal with earlier in the evening.

I sighed loudly and stared at my cards. Stared at my chips—or lack of them. Stared at the empty spot on the scarred table where my wad of cash had been before I lost it all. I was worse than flat busted, I was in the hole, and needed a big win just to get out of the game alive.

I glanced at the door. Still no sign of Lucky. And I was running out of time.

With another heavy sigh, I reached into my coat pocket and slowly—reluctantly—pulled out my last hope. My special hip flask.

I stared into its polished surface and saw one shit-faced son of a bitch staring back at me. As my poker buddies studied me, I slowly caressed the bottle as if it were a magic lamp. But alas, no genie appeared to save my ass.

I hugged it to my chest one last time, kissed it

good-bye, then laid it reverently on the table. "It's solid silver," I whispered.

P.J. grabbed it to confirm its value. He squinted at the inscription, his lips moving as he read. Then he guffawed and read it out loud in a girlish voice: "'To dodging bullets. Love, Jane.'"

Well, I thought they'd never stop laughing. Mickey was getting off making kissy sounds. But at last P.J. tossed it into the pot, keeping me in the game for one more hand. We were just hunkering down for the final skirmish when the door crashed open.

"WHAT THE FUCK IS *THIS*?" a voice thundered like the wrath of God.

The game screeched to a dead halt. A definite chill fell upon the room.

It wasn't hard to tell that the infamous Lucky had finally arrived.

"Looks like you're done, pal," Mickey said, his voice low and urgent. "Thanks for the memories."

I raised my head, hard luck and disappointment written all over my face. Then I narrowed my eyes at the big man. He definitely beat the pants off Curtis in the "Badass Motherfucker" category. By far the most dangerous man in the room.

Or was he . . . ?

I squinted, trying to hold his gaze. "You're Lucky?" I drawled.

"Yeah," he grunted, expecting me to run like hell. But I didn't. I just sat there, waiting.

He stared at me, head cocked in curiosity. Maybe halfway impressed that I had the balls not to cower like a flower girl in his presence. "What is it, kid?" he asked. "You looking for a job?"

I slowly shook my head. "You *are* the job."

"Huh?" Lucky was obviously confused.

So I straightened up, stone-cold sober, to explain.

But my mama always told me that actions speak louder than words. That's when I threw back my chair, stood up, and let my favorite move articulate my meaning:

1. *Start with two loaded, silenced pistols.*
2. *Cross-draw from opposite pockets.*
3. *Remember what the bastard did to deserve this.*
4. *Pull triggers.*

I fired both guns and blasted Lucky against the wall.

Guess they wouldn't be calling him "Lucky" anymore.

My new poker buddies suddenly realized that they'd underestimated me—that maybe, just maybe, *I* was the most dangerous badass motherfucker in the room.

Curtis groped for his semi, but gosh darn it, I'd just had to relieve him of it before the last hand had been dealt. Just in case. It was lying somewhere under my chair.

"Go big or go home, y'all!" I shouted, using a little poker lingo to wrap things up.

Then I eliminated the other players from the game.

Which reminded me—my cards were still on the table. I turned them over and tapped my hand. "Pair of threes."

Not a great hand. But in this case, I guess it would do, since I was the only player who hadn't folded.

All good things must come to an end, so I reached toward the pot for my winnings. I didn't take back any of my money, though—it was just petty cash from my office, anyway.

I took the only thing of value in the whole damn room: my silver flask.

Then left Curtis's semi in its place, just in case he had any heirs.

To avoid the party up front, I slipped out the rear exit into the back alley.

The rats snickered in the shadows. But the moon peeked down at me in between the run-down buildings, reminding me that there were still things of beauty in the world, like stars in the sky.

I drew out my flask and caught some of the silver moonlight on its polished surface. Took a long comforting drink. Guess it had gotten me through another night of dodging bullets.

Then I spotted my ride home: a monster motorcycle gleaming in the shadows, with a license plate that said LUCKY.

Yeah, well, who was lucky now?

I jumped on, fired up the engine, and got the hell out of the neighborhood.

Just another night out with the boys.

JANE

Have you been a bad boy, Marco? Have you?"

The bed shook as my client nodded like a wimpy little child.

What an idiot, I couldn't help but think.

Trussed up like a Thanksgiving turkey with a rubber ball in his mouth, the great, powerful, wealthy Marco Racin looked completely ridiculous.

And he was entirely under my control.

Scumbag. I didn't know whether to laugh or throw up.

I snapped my whip in front of his eyes. "You know what happens to bad boys, don't you? They get *punished.* Is that what you want?" Marco whined like a baby.

I fondled the whip. "You like the taste of leather?"

He nodded, almost wild with desire.

I slid slowly onto the bed beside Marco, drawing out the torture. I felt him tremble with excitement and fear.

"Have you been having impure thoughts?" I whispered in his ear.

He nodded, yes, yes!

"Have you been abusing your body?"

He nodded, more frantically—yes, yes, *yes*!

Time to take the game to the next level. I checked the exits, then smiled. What I said after that would come as a complete surprise to my date. But then again, didn't the experts always say that a little surprise kept a relationship interesting?

"Have you violated international law, baby?" I demanded, my voice now velvet-encased steel. "Tell me you haven't."

Marco's eyes widened, and I saw a bead of sweat roll down his big fat nose.

I cracked my whip, and delivered the bombshell. "Have you been selling big weapons to bad people?"

That's when various parts of the great Marco Racin's anatomy went as limp as overcooked spaghetti.

He tried to yell for his bodyguards. But of course he couldn't with that silly rubber ball stuffed in his mouth.

I pulled his reddening face back, pressing my hands into his cheeks. Then, without warning, I gave his head an efficient twist.

Marco's eyes bulged. The little ball popped out of his mouth and rolled across the floor. His days playing games with other people's lives had finally come to an end.

As Marco's lifeless body slumped to the bed, I reached into my coat for my cell phone to check the time. It was already 8:30. "Damn. The Colemans."

John would kill me if I didn't show.

Just then I heard a tentative knock on the door. One of Marco's bodyguards, nervous about interrupting the fun and games.

"Mr. Racin," he called hesitantly through the crack in the door. "We have a plane in an hour, sir . . . Sir?"

As the pounding on the door increased, I decided I'd better slip away from this party fast, so I didn't have to explain what had happened to my "host."

I raced out onto the terrace, scanned the rooftop for guards—saw none—then peered down over the railing.

Some fifty floors below me, the city's taxis swam like bright fish in a black river. I needed to catch one before Marco's men made me the Catch of the Day.

But I'd come prepared. My black leather bag had been designed for bad days like this. Calmly I strode back to the doors to the hotel suite, hooked one end of my purse on a metal wall sconce, then turned to face the night sky.

Lovely view, I thought briefly, then ran toward the edge.

Should work.

Behind me, I heard Marco's men finally burst into the room, firing their weapons.

Time to say adieu.

"Thanks for the nudge, boys," I whispered, then took a flying leap over the railing.

To the stunned guards, it must have appeared as if I'd simply thrown myself off the roof like some kind of suicide assassin.

But as I plunged toward the ground, the fabric of my bag unraveled into a superthin almost invisible black Kevlar cord, which I rode like a spider all the way to the ground below.

Definitely the smartest bag I'd ever carried.

When I neared street level, I let go and dropped to the sidewalk. A passing pedestrian stopped and gawked.

Must be a tourist, I thought. A regular New Yorker would never have blinked. But I wasn't worried. By the time this guy told friends, he'd have convinced himself he'd seen a movie being shot on location. Or at least I hoped so, because I sure didn't have time to stop and explain.

With a smile, I snapped my overcoat closed and walked toward the front of the hotel as if I were just an ordinary housewife walking home from the corner market.

Without breaking my stride, I approached the doorman just as a cab pulled up at the curb. I slid into the backseat, tipped the doorman with my warmest smile, and said, "Thanks, sweetie."

"My pleasure, ma'am," he replied, and meant it.

After a quick "mission accomplished" call to headquarters on my cell phone, I sat back and relaxed for the first time since I got the assignment.

God, I was dying to take a shower. With lots of hot water and soap to wash the slime of the world off my skin.

It wouldn't do much for the way I felt inside, though.

I leaned my head against the glass and tried to look between the skyscrapers for some stars.

But the only stars you could find in this part of town were the ones driving by in limos.

So I closed my eyes and conjured up my own.

They looked a lot like the ones I'd seen one night in Bogotá.

JOHN

I remembered the Colemans' party on the way home.
   Wow, the fun just never ends.

But we'd said we'd be there, and it was important to be good neighbors.

As I entered the foyer, I heard Jane upstairs in

our room—home from "work." So I headed up to remind her about the party.

I won't say I snuck up on her, but let's just say I didn't go out of my way to announce my arrival.

As I paused in the doorway, I saw her struggling to button up a pink dress. Something looked odd about her movements, but I couldn't quite put my finger on what it was.

Suddenly she froze, like a deer picking up the scent of a hunter, and turned. "Honey," she said—with a tense, forced smile. "Didn't see you downstairs."

"Just got home." My eyes lingered on hers. "How was that work thing?"

She shrugged coolly. "Fine, good."

As she walked toward me, she sniffed—her nose wrinkling in disapproval—then she frowned. "Another one with Eddie?"

"Went by the sports bar," I lied casually. "Put a few bucks on the game."

"How'd you do?" Jane asked.

I thought back over my evening and shrugged. "I got lucky."

I know. Puns are the lowest form of humor. But hey, a guy has to amuse himself when he can't exactly rely on scintillating conversation with his wife.

She walked past me, out of the room. Careful to leave paper-thin spaces between us.

That little dance we do. It's called the Miserable Marriage Sidestep.

I followed her downstairs, snagged a bottle of wine as I passed through the kitchen. Glad, actually, that we were headed over to the Colemans'.

Shooting the breeze over a few drinks might be just what the doctor ordered right now.

"Everything okay at the office?" I asked as we climbed the steps to the Colemans' front porch—looking like the perfect American couple.

"Fine, good" was all she said. It was all she ever said about her job. "How was the ball game?"

"Awesome," I replied automatically. "Knicks by one in overtime."

"The Knicks played tonight?" she asked me, fussing with my hair the way she does sometimes, and I frowned.

"Yeah—*hey!*" I said, flattening it back in place, worried about the Knicks now, trying to remember the schedule. *They did play tonight, didn't they?*

Fortunately, the door opened, and Martin and Suzy appeared, beaming like we were their oldest, dearest friends. "Welcome, neighbors!"

"Hey!" I said, hoping our smiles didn't look too fake.

Jane and I stayed together long enough to have drinks shoved into our hands and to put in an appearance as perfect spouses. Then we drifted, hopping from one conversation to the next. I made my way around a plastered guest who was playing the baby grand—it was either "Stairway to Heaven" or the *Moonlight* Sonata, I couldn't quite tell. Then I ran aground in the cigar fog created by a group of investment bankers speaking the language of stocks and bonds.

"Are you kidding?" one of them said. "Duxbury's never going to close that high. I heard their stock's getting butchered."

"It's a bloodbath," another one confirmed. "John, how'd you make out this quarter? You take a beating?"

Okay, someone was talking to me. I rewound to the

question. "Actually," I said, jerking a thumb in the general direction of my home next door, "I got all my dough buried under the shed over there."

Which they thought was pretty damn funny—lots of guffaws and backslapping. For half a second I was tempted to show them what else I had tucked away under that innocuous-looking structure, but I wasn't drunk enough, and neither were they.

A condition I decided I definitely needed to remedy.

JANE

When I got home from work, it was just past nine. No time to shower and change, so I just pulled a loose pink dress from my "Suburban Wife" collection on over the little black dominatrix number I'd been wearing.

Just as I was buttoning up the dress, my inner security alarm went off. I quickly ID'd the intruder in the dresser mirror.

John—lounging in the doorway, studying me. He scared the life out of me, actually. How'd he do that? *Nobody* sneaks up on Jane Smith.

And what kind of man sneaks up on his wife like that, anyway?

How long had he been there? Had he seen what I was wearing underneath my respectable pink dress?

We danced around each other—doing the His 'n Her Shuffle long-married couples are known to perfect—exchanged some passive-aggressive barbs, then headed next door to the Colemans'. Sometimes I dreaded their parties, but that night I was glad to have a place to escape to.

As we walked up the steps, John kept asking me about work. Weird, since he rarely took an interest anymore. I tried hard not to break a sweat, but that proved nearly impossible wearing as much leather under my country-club attire as I was. To cover up my nervousness, I mumbled something about the ball game and fiddled with his hair, which only made him scowl.

But as soon as the Colemans opened the door, we were wearing our matching his-'n'-her, happy-couple smiles.

As our hosts led us into the party and poured us drinks, I couldn't help but wonder: *What am I doing here?*

All these people that we saw at barbecues and holiday parties. The men slapping John on the back, the women greeting me with air kisses and cutesy waves.

They think we're the perfect couple, I thought as I smiled and kissed back. The women adored John and envied me; the men winked and called John a lucky son of a bitch, and sometimes tried to corner me in the kitchen.

If they only knew we were just Barbie and Ken, and that our dream house was nothing but a plastic facade.

But maybe I was just tired. Assignments like Marco Racin sometimes depressed me—I preferred the straight shoot.

And this wasn't *just* my cover; this was my life, these were my neighbors. Nice people, most of them, if a little on the boring side. This was the perfect world I'd dreamed of as a child.

So maybe it was the fact that I was still wearing my black leather dominatrix clothes beneath my dress that was making me feel as if I didn't fit in. A "double life" to most of these other women meant stepping outside their role as wife and mother to serve as PTA president. What would they think if they knew what I really did for a living?

As usual, John had quickly abandoned me and was off shooting the breeze with all the other half-crocked husbands, while I was left to swap recipes, potty-training tips, and neighborhood gossip with the wives.

So I stood there, talking to three women whose party accessories included a baby in their arms.

Mom number one was fawning over her little darling as if it were the first girl ever born on the planet.

I smothered a laugh when her "perfect" baby spit up all over her "perfect" pantsuit.

But Mom number one just smiled indulgently and glanced at me. "Hold her a sec while I run and clean up?"

What—?

Mom number one had suddenly shoved her baby into my arms.

Nothing that had happened to me during my evening at the hotel had scared me half as much as this. "No, really, I . . ."

But Mom had already disappeared.

I held my breath and stared down at the squirming little bundle. Guns, I could handle. Men *acting* like babies—a piece of cake. But real-live babies—I didn't even know how to hold them. *Please, God,* I thought, *don't let me break it!*

For a moment the little girl and I stared each other down; she seemed as stunned as I was to be thrust into this unexpected relationship. Perhaps she could tell I was not the mothering type.

I don't do babies. No big deal. It's a choice I had to make a long time ago. I'd never had anyone to depend on, and I chose a life that meant I couldn't afford to have someone depend on me. Two A.M. feedings and staying home with sick children would never fit into my schedule. Never mind the fact that I risked my life every time I walked out that door.

Couldn't do that to a kid.

The other mothers didn't see it that way. I was a young married woman, living in the burbs, *without* a baby. I could see the questions in their eyes every month I showed up not pregnant. Especially with a husband like John.

"Babies see everything, you know," Mom number two was saying.

"Mmm-hmm," Mom number three agreed. "It's as if they can see into your very soul."

Terrific, I thought. I peeked at the foreign operative in my arms as she sized me up. Could this tiny spy really read my thoughts? Could she look into my core and see what I'd done an hour ago with the very hands that now cradled her?

As the mothers looked on, I smiled weakly, waiting for Judge Baby to hand down a sentence for the lifestyle I've been leading.

And then . . . she smiled at me.

The little assassin!

For a moment I couldn't breathe. I felt as if I'd been shot in the heart with a stun gun.

"She likes you," Suzy said, peeking over my shoulder.

I let out my breath and smiled at the darling little girl. *Thanks for not blowing my cover, kiddo.*

I felt relieved. And something else—a strange feeling I couldn't quite describe.

Then, just to yank my chain, the little stinker pulled at the top button on my pink dress, revealing a scrap of the black leather sin suit beneath.

I quickly covered it up and glanced around, hoping no one had seen.

Fortunately the moms' attention had been drawn to some new knickknack on Suzy's whatnot. But I definitely felt a distant pair of eyes on me. *Who . . . ?*

I scanned the crowd and spotted him, through a haze of cigar smoke.

John, staring at me, watching me with the baby.

Strange. I'd never seen him look so scared.

We left the party soon after that. I claimed a headache; John apologized that he had a big meeting in the morning.

Moments later we were back in our lovely home, in lovely pajamas, brushing our teeth at our lovely his-and-her sinks. Our faces in the twin mirrors reminded me of the dead-eyed portraits of people from hundreds of years ago that hang in museums.

The sounds of flossing and brushing seemed overly loud in the silence.

John spit, rubbed his eye. I glanced at him, this man with whom I shared so many of the ordinary but intimate activities of daily life. This stranger.

I couldn't for the life of me have guessed what he was thinking about. It was a mystery.

But not the good kind.

I met a man once, a mysterious stranger—a man who danced along the knife edge of danger and never looked back, except to take my hand and pull me along with him.

But when I tried to hold on to him—when I married him—he disappeared.

If he'd ever been real at all.

John glanced up and caught me staring. I gave him a tight smile.

We went to bed.

The lights went out.

I pulled the covers up to my chin and turned away from my husband. Maybe, if I looked, I could still find that man in my dreams.

I don't know if I slept. But lying on my side, facing away from John, I seemed to watch the seconds of my life click away on the digital clock, the minutes passing like hours.

11:15. 12:04. 1:37 . . .

3:00.

Suddenly two phones rang. His-and-her cell phones.

John and I sat up instantly and swung away from each other.

Had he been awake all this time, too?

Both bedside lamps clicked on. We sat on the edge of the mattress like mirror images and answered our phones.

"Jane Smith."

"John Smith."

On my phone, a man's voice. Elegant accent. It was my boss. Code name: Father. I could picture him in his stark, darkened office; I imagined him sitting there every moment of the day or night, never sleeping, his mind always tinkering with some new plot.

"It's three in the morning," I said softly. "Everything okay . . . Dad?"

A new assignment. Urgent. Father gave me instructions: simple, direct, no chitchat. No "How are you?" No "Did I wake you?" No "Say hello to your husband for me."

"Yeah. Okay. Of course," I said.

There was a click on the line. No good-bye.

Behind me, I heard John speaking into his own cell phone.

"This is the second time this week," he whispered. A long pause, then: "Right. I understand. No problem."

I heard him end the call with a soft *click.*

We sat there in silence a moment. I could hear John thinking.

We turned toward each other at the same time.

"What's up?" John asked lightly.

"Oh, Dad's not well," I said, trying to sound concerned. "Mom's freaked, thinks he's got pneumonia." I shrugged. "Probably just a cough."

John thought a moment. "Well," he said carefully. "Maybe you should take the day off, go see if the old man's okay."

I studied his face in the soft light.

Why was he being so nice?

"Your mom would love it," he went on, "if you spent the night at their house."

And so would you? I wanted to ask. But instead I said, "You're so sweet."

John shrugged. "Just thinking of your dad."

I nodded. Sure he was. Then: "What was yours?"

"Atlanta office," he answered quickly. Too quickly. "Got an e-mail about the stress statistics for that dam." He shrugged again. "I'm gonna be working flat out next couple days anyway."

We both nodded, satisfied.

I'd bought his story; he'd bought mine.

Like dancers in a well-rehearsed ballet, we reached for our bedside lamps, turned out the lights, and slid back under the covers.

"That damn dam," I whispered in the darkness.

"Yeah," he said. "That damn dam."

I closed my eyes and lay there in the darkness, hands on my chest like a corpse in a coffin. And I could feel John doing the same.

Slowly, but surely, we were burying each other alive.

JOHN

Dawn—my favorite hour. As the world tips between night and day. Darkness and light. The past and the future.

For that brief time anything seems possible.

Suitcase in hand, I whistled as I crossed the back lawn to the toolshed, just like any happy husband getting ready to go to work.

Once inside, I locked the door and stopped whistling.

The toolshed was just a cover for the real tools of my trade.

As usual, the grinding bench skidded aside easily to reveal a safety box in the floor. I worked the combo lock, unlatched a trapdoor handle, then spun the handle.

The floor opened up.

I clambered down the ladder, pulling the suitcase

in after me, then switched on the light and considered the possibilities. The stacks of cash I kept there were neatly organized according to country of issue.

Choice of weapon was a little tougher. Too many damn options. My weapon collection was a virtual arsenal: rocket launchers, grenades, and handguns galore. It was like shopping at Wal-Mart.

I needed something light and easily concealed, but with dependable firepower and range. I found what I wanted, then quickly locked up.

Back topside, I was Happy Hubby again. Whistling, I headed into the garage, locked my suitcase in the trunk of the sedan, and backed out into the street, my mind already focused on my work.

Automatically checking the rearview, I realized I'd forgotten one husbandly duty.

I hit the automatic garage-door opener, and the garage door slowly closed.

Then I drove off to my other life.

JANE

I was still in bed, but my eyes were open; I was alert, listening.

Then it came: a sedan pulling out of the driveway. *Don't forget to close the garage door, John.*

Okay, there it was, that unmistakable sound of the door closing. He'd remembered for a change.

I rolled out of bed and dashed for the bathroom. I didn't have much time.

Four minutes to shower, three to dress—hey, I was a professional—I dashed into the kitchen and switched my oven to CLEAN.

No, I wasn't an obsessive housewife who couldn't bear to leave the house with drippings from last night's lasagna baked onto the oven floor. I had something else cooking in my kitchen.

The timer beeped, and I yanked open the range door. Next I typed in several digits on the touch pad and . . .

Beep! A ten-second warning began.

I tapped in my security code, and the beeping stopped. The base of my oven slid open.

And I smiled.

This is where I kept my *special* kitchen gadgets: sleek guns, glistening knives. Clean, well oiled, and organized.

Since John couldn't even boil water, I'd quickly learned that the best place to store a few secrets was in the kitchen.

I looked through my choices, then slid my favorite knife onto my thigh.

Lights off, coffeepot unplugged, and I was out the door, into the garage, backing out of the driveway in my car with the "Neighborhood Watch: Keeping Our Streets Safe" bumper sticker.

It's what I did each day, though it was not quite the line of work my neighbors imagined.

Soon I was at a high-rise building in the city, shoving through the revolving door. As I moved through the atrium and waited for the elevator, I checked my appearance in the mirrored doors: formfitting black suit, short skirt, high heels, briefcase.

Killer outfit. I was ready to go to work.

The elevator swept me to my office on an upper floor, and I stepped into the security air lock. Ultraviolet light washed over me, checking for weapons and verifying my identity.

My company logo appeared on a security monitor, along with a readout of my body temperature, blood pressure, weapons, jewelry. They could probably even type what brand of mascara I was wearing.

"Jane Smith," said a female computer voice. "Confirmed."

I reached for the door to my office, but the voice stopped me: "Stand by for contact."

I paused, surprised. This was unusual. And then a face appeared on the screen.

A familiar, distinguished-looking man, the Big Boss.

Father.

"Sorry to intrude," Father said with formality. "But we have a . . . *situation*. And I need you to handle it personally."

My eyes narrowed. This was *not* normal procedure.

"Target?" I asked.

My newest hit appeared on the screen.

"Benjamin Danz," Father explained. "I'm sending the specs now. We need this *quick, clean,* and *contained.*"

I nodded. "I'm on it, sir."

I reached for the door to go to work, but Father's voice stopped me.

"Jane . . ."

I looked to the screen.

He paused a moment, then said only: "Good luck."

My eyes narrowed. That was very, *very* uncharacteristic. Father was usually brief and efficient. And in spite of my long relationship with the firm, he rarely wasted time on social amenities.

So what was different about today? The expression on his face . . . there was something odd about it. But before I could study him further, his image disappeared from the screen.

I shook my head. Probably just imagining things.

With my ID confirmed, the far door opened, and I stepped into the high-security offices of Triple-Click—a top computer temp agency. But that was only a front.

I stopped a moment and looked around. God, I loved this place! This vast ultrasecure metal room buzzed with the world's most advanced technology—flooding data, live feeds, all at warp speed and humming with efficiency.

But more important was the staff I'd assembled. In a male-dominated industry, I'd gone out of my way to hire the smartest, most competent young women I could find.

I smiled at Jasmine, who ran this place—at least, until I arrived.

"Good morning, girls, how's our day look?"

Jasmine tapped a key on her computer, and a huge plasma-screen monitor lit up with our logo and specs on our new target, direct from the home office.

Yep. Father worked fast.

"Okay, ladies," I said briskly. "Let's get to work."

Our newest target appeared on the screen—photo, stats, daily habits, everything but the last time he'd gone to the john.

"Target is being moved tonight across the Canadian border to a federal facility," I informed my staff. A map appeared, and I pointed to the relevant location. "Only vulnerability is here, just south of the border. Julie, I want GPS and SAT elly of the canyon, and weather report for the last three days," I said to my go-to gal for stats.

God, this felt good. My job was all I needed: It eliminated the confusion and self-doubt I'd felt the night before—first at the party, then at home—the way sunshine burned off morning fog. I had a job to do, and I knew how to do it. I was in my element; *this* was home.

Everything seemed possible in the morning.

I studied the man's face in the photos. *Cute.*

I knew that shouldn't matter. A mark was a mark. But somehow it was easier if the slime was as ugly as hell. I don't know, maybe it was just a girl thing, but to me, it was always a little harder to assassinate a guy who was good looking.

But no problem here. It wasn't like he was Brad Pitt or anything.

I studied that face, memorizing every line, every wart, the length of his eyelashes, the shape of his ears—branding his name into my memory.

Benjamin Danz.

Well, Mr. Danz, welcome to the last day of your life...

JOHN

I parked outside an anonymous building on the waterfront, then slipped into a small office on the ground floor labeled SMITH ENGINEERING, where, as far as the general public knew, I was just another guy running a worldwide engineering enterprise.

"Morning, Louise," I said to my receptionist. She and her husband Louie manned the front office. They were a happy, comfortable twosome, almost like a mom and dad to me. But I pitied any evildoer who underestimated their abilities.

They were secretary, valet, and bodyguard all rolled into one, and I treated them like royalty. Besides, Louise made the best chocolate-chip cookies on the planet. I definitely had to stay on her good side.

"Morning, Mr. Smith," Louise replied. "Trouble in Atlanta?"

"That's what I'm told."

Louie handed me an envelope. "Airline boarding-pass stub, taxi receipts, hotel bills."

"And we've got those new specs for the dam," Louise added, handing me a rolled-up blueprint.

"Good, good, I'll take a look," I said as I headed down the hall toward my office.

Halfway there, Eddie emerged from his own hole in

the wall and fell in step beside me. He was singing some pop ditty, goofing around as usual.

I shook my head. "Eddie, what's new?" I asked him, as much to stop the assault on my ears as to gather information.

"Same old same old. People need killing." He shrugged, then added, "You know, I'm having a little get-together this weekend. Barbecue at the house. Just the guys."

"Yeah, okay, I'll check with Jane," I said, and headed toward my office.

Eddie shook his head as he watched me go. "Uh-huh. You wanna borrow my cell phone, John? I'm just saying in case you want to scratch your ass or take a piss or something, you should probably check with your wife first . . ."

I just rolled my eyes and closed the door without answering. I didn't need marriage advice from a guy who still lived with his mother.

Inside my office—Smith Engineering's secure room—was where the real work got done. The sparse midcentury decorating suited me. The place felt comfortable, un-cluttered, efficient. Like something out of an early James Bond movie. Here I could find my focus; I could think. This was home.

The door closed. The room was secure.

I dropped the rolled-up blueprint into a pile of blueprints that had never been opened, never been read. Then I sat down at my desk and pulled the arm on a model crane.

Instantly a panel on the wall shifted to reveal a high-tech plasma screen, displaying our agency's dark logo.

"Good morning," I said.

"Voiceprint confirm," a secretary, voice only, replied. "Good morning, Mr. Smith."

Then a face appeared, that of an elegant dark-haired woman whose considerable years in the business were reflected in her eyes.

It was the big kahuna. My boss. Otherwise known as Atlanta.

One look from her could turn the most ruthless operative into a sniveling little boy.

I straightened slightly, surprised to see her.

"Hello, John," Atlanta said in her black velvet voice. "Quite a body count this week."

I'll take that as a compliment, I thought, but said nothing.

"We've got a Priority One," she went on, "so I need your expertise."

A target profile flickered on screen: photo, stats, everything but the last time the guy took a crap.

They probably had that info, too, somewhere.

"Target's name is Danz," Atlanta reported. "Aka the Tank."

"The Tank . . ." I almost laughed. "He looks fourteen."

Oops. Atlanta's face tightened. She was deadly serious about this, whatever it was. I better behave myself.

"He's a direct threat to the firm," Atlanta continued with an edge to her voice. "DIA custody, They're making a ground-to-air handoff to helo, ten miles north of the Mexican border. I want you on-site, make sure that target does *not* change hands."

I leaned forward to study the data streaming across the screen. People can lie, cheat, pretend to be something they're not. But the eyes always give them away.

One look at them and I knew instantly that this guy was a total jerk.

Benjamin Danz, I thought, *welcome to the last day of your life . . .*

JANE

I'd set up operations in an old dusty mine shack perched on a rocky precipice somewhere in the desert.

Where exactly? God only knew—somewhere north of the U.S.-Mexican border was the best I could tell you.

I scoped out the area with binoculars, and saw nothing but miles and miles of hot burning sand.

And yet its haunting beauty tore at my heart somehow. The lonely emptiness of it all . . .

Wait—what was that?

Ah. An incoming dust cloud led my eye to a convoy of SUVs, shimmering in the sun as they traveled along a nearly invisible sand-swept road that snaked across the desert.

"Target incoming," I reported to my team, who were in touch by radio.

"Copy that," Jasmine answered.

I grinned. Time to go to work.

Here was the setup: I'd connected a fairly simple triggered timer box to mining cables running out into the desert floor.

That area was defined on my laptop by a wire-frame image with twenty white dots: a wide kill zone through which the caravan would pass.

It was kind of like a roach motel.

The convoy would check in—*blam!*—but they wouldn't check out.

I waited for my prey to move closer, then set the plan in motion. "Charges set," I reported. "Arming on contact."

The images on the screen told me the good news: The convoy was heading straight for my kill zone. One minute away.

Perfect.

"Right on time," I murmured, and smiled.

Careful planning, perfect positioning, flawless teamwork . . .

I figured we'd wrap the job and be out of there before the desert heat could wilt our powder-fresh antiperspirants.

Easy as pie.

But then something ruined the view.

Bloody hell! What was that?

I adjusted my binoculars. Nothing but sand.

Then—there it was again!

Now I could see: Some kind of small sports vehicle—I think they called it a Baja Buggy. It bounced over a sand dune, disappeared, crested another dune . . .

Then vanished again into silence.

Then again. And again. "What the hell is that?" Jasmine exclaimed in my headset. "Threat? Redundancy?"

I shook my head in disgust. "Maybe just some yahoo in a dune buggy. Desert's full of them."

As the vehicle moved closer, I caught sight of the driver. He was wearing a helmet and goggles, a silly scarf flapping in the breeze behind him. He looked like he was having the time of his life.

Fucking asshole.

Of all the sandboxes in the world, he had to come play in mine.

I checked my screen and scowled. The buggy showed up as a moving blinking dot on my laptop screen.

He was headed straight into my kill zone.

Goddamn son of a . . .

"He's going to set off the charges."

I tensed, waiting. "Stop . . . stop . . . stop . . ."

Mere inches short of the laser trigger, the buggy halted. I exhaled a breath I didn't realize I was holding.

Now, if he would just get the hell out of there . . .

But then the driver pulled a hotshot spin, slewing sideways—barely, just barely slicing into the kill zone with his back tire.

Like a lot of things in life, *just barely* was as good as 100 percent.

My computer flashed its warning: green—meaning, the charges were activated. Thirty seconds to go.

"Countdown initiated," I heard Jasmine exclaim. "Are they in the zone?! Jane!"

"No, no, it's gonna blow too early!" I cried. "I've got to reroute the charges!"

I lunged toward my timer box and went to work, disconnecting wires, trying to take back orders it had been programmed to execute no matter what. It was intense intricate work—not the kind of thing I liked to do in a rush.

Head down, focused, I broke out in a sweat.

At last I managed to defuse the charges. The lights turned white.

I looked up to check on my gate-crasher.

He'd parked his toy and hopped out. He was looking around. And then I watched him open a silver case. A weapons system perhaps?

No . . . a lunch box? Who the hell was this? An enemy operative—or a happy hiker?

"What is this guy doing?" I muttered. I watched in amazement as the man pulled out a wrapped sandwich and what looked like pie.

Helluva place to stop and have a damn picnic! Whoever he was, he was skipping the Skippy and going straight for dessert.

JOHN

Good afternoon, Mr. Danz," I said, watching an approaching convoy of cars. Through my binoculars, I estimated their distance at about a half mile.

We were in the desert somewhere, a little north of the Mexican border.

Stationed atop a high dune, I had an excellent view of the road. The position of the convoy allowed me just enough time to open my lunch box and grab my sandwich and slice of key lime pie. Both were wrapped so tightly in Saran Wrap, they looked like they were about to suffocate.

That's my little Martha Stewart, Jane.

God, when had she gotten so uptight?

A Post-it note stuck to the sandwich said: *XOXO Jane*. Nice of her to make food for me. Nice to include the note. Only . . . she'd put a thousand of these in a thousand lunches, and they always said the same thing. I almost wondered if she had them printed up at Kinko's.

I unwrapped the pie first. Hey, it was pretty good pie, I didn't want to hurry through it if the convoy got here quicker than estimated.

Damn, it was hotter than the devil's own sauna out here—I sure could use a couple of margaritas. As I surveyed the approaching motorcade, I pulled out my silver flask, sneaked a belt of Red Label, and tried to pretend it was icy-cold tequila.

Then I took a big bite of dessert—and moaned.

Mmm—damn good pie. One of the few things Jane made that I actually liked. It reminded me of hot nights in foreign places. Like the Caribbean. Or Bogotá. The sharp tang of lime went perfect with the scotch.

But I'd better keep my mind on my work. I mean, this was an easy hit, as far as hits go: well set up, plenty of time. Yet I still needed to focus. Even when it came to the smallest assignments, I prided myself on doing a perfect job.

But there was no reason why I couldn't have a little fun.

"So," I said like a sportscaster, "we got us a hefty convoy of vehicles. Main attraction is a heavily armed Navigator center stage. A tough can to open. Any ideas, John?"

I heaved a Javelin CLU 76mm rocket launcher onto my shoulder. "Well, Bob," I answered myself, playing the coanchor, "I thought I'd try my luck with the Javelin."

I activated the laser sight, searching for my target.

"Incorporating passive target acquisition with an integrated thermal imaging sight. It's got all the features you'd expect from a larger fire-and-forget weapon system wrapped up in an easily portable six-point-four-kg package."

The convoy moved closer.

Benjamin Danz was about to die.

I sneaked another bite of pie.

JANE

*a*ll my questions were put to rest when I saw Dune Buggy Dude hoisting a huge rocket launcher onto his shoulder. This guy was hunting, babe— but not roadrunners or armadillo. Dammit! He was after *my* guy!

I did not like this. I did not like this one bit! I plan a perfect little hit, and some two-bit James Bond wannabe stumbles onto my playground waving his big toy gun in my face!

Dammit! Dammit! Dammit!

My voice was hard and controlled when I alerted my crew: "Its not a yahoo. We've got another player on the field."

There was a pause; I knew Jasmine was studying my live feeds. And I knew what she was thinking. Hell, we'd memorized the same page in assassin school.

In a situation like this, the book said to abort.

Dammit! Dammit! Dammit!

I could hear the seconds ticking away. Could hear Jasmine biting her tongue, trying hard not to give advice.

Frantically I considered my options. Then I saw that our intruder was preparing to fire—*now!*—

"He's going to take out the target before they hit the kill zone," Jasmine blurted.

That's what *she* thought.

"No, he's not," I said.

Not if I had anything to do with it.

All discussion ceased.

Time to move—*now.*

I swung a silenced survival rifle from a sling on my back and snapped it into firing position.

As Buggy Boy took aim at his target, I locked onto mine: HIM.

Thanks for holding still, dude . . .
I *fired*.

JOHN

This was gonna be so easy.

I had my Javelin locked onto my target. I was pumped, but relaxed. And the convoy was walking right into my hands.

I even had a moment to spare.

It should have been a piece of cake. Or should I say pie?

Because that's when Jane's key lime pie began calling my name again.

Some of Jane's cooking flat-out sucks—not that I ever tell *her* that. Hell, I take enough risks every day in my job without doing something really crazy like that at home. Besides, traveling the world, I've eaten a lot worse.

But this pie of hers rocked.

I checked my sights. I had just enough time left. I smiled as I reached for that last sweet-and-sour bite.

Hey! There was sand getting into my pie!

I reached down to cover it.

Phhhzzzzzt!!

"What the—"

Lucky for me, my well-trained body was ahead of my brain. I ate sand as I hit the ground. Then I just lay there for a moment, afraid to reach up, afraid to feel if my head was still there.

But slowly I realized I was just grazed. My right

ear stung like hell, though. The bullet had clipped it. My ear was bleeding, but not too much.

Now I was pissed.

Somebody was out there.

Somebody who wanted me dead.

JANE

Player down," I reported to my crew. "Back in business."

That was easy enough. One shot, and he was no longer an annoying interruption to my game.

I like to think I'm the kind of person who's open to discussion on most topics. But when I'm in the middle of a job, hey—

Don't mess with Jane.

Too bad Pie Boy had to learn the hard way.

But the great thing about the desert?

No muss. No fuss. No cleanup. The buzzards would take care of that.

I cracked my knuckles, and turned my attention back to the approaching convoy.

JOHN

I searched the area where I thought the shot had originated. I saw nothing but an abandoned mine shack.

But wait. *Movement—there.* A slim figure passed by the open doorway.

Somebody was there, and up to something. Looked like a little guy. Whatever he had planned, he definitely didn't want me snooping around.

Out here in the desert, there was nowhere to run, nowhere to hide.

Only one option: Eliminate the threat.

I dusted off my launcher and took dead aim at the shack.

I fired it up, and watched it cough out a heat-seeking warhead. Thirty feet ahead, it roared to life, spewing out a sheet of flame while screaming across the desert toward whoever had the misfortune of being in that shack.

Whoa, Mama. Do it!

JANE

J had a teacher once in seventh grade. She used to nag me about my lack of focus.

If she could only see me now.

Every fiber of my being was focused on the approaching convoy. I could visualize Benjamin Danz riding like a prince in that SUV.

I'd done my homework, and I was ready to ace the test.

But then an unexpected noise broke my concentration. It sounded something like *whooomph!*

As in . . .

MAJOR FREAKIN' FIREPOWER!

A quick glance told me it was headed for my current address. The shack.

Shit!

A blazing fireball was hurtling straight at me. And I was gonna eat it!

By instinct, I dived off the rocks . . .

JOHN

*B*oom! The old mine shack exploded into a million pieces.

I gulped and stared down in awe at the smoking object I held in my hand.

"You should *so* not be allowed to buy these . . ."

I guess I had successfully eliminated my intruder. Unfortunately the kick-ass blast had also announced my presence to my target.

The convoy had stopped, alerted to danger. And now it was turning around . . .

Oh, no you don't!

I still had a chance to pull this thing off.

I quickly hoisted my trusty rocket launcher to my shoulder and took aim again.

JANE

The force of the explosion propelled me through the air. I hit the ground hard, losing my gun in the fall.

My laptop, I thought as I tumbled away from the exploding mine shack.

Yeah, lost that, too. If I could just find it . . . could I still pull this off? Or was it destroyed in the blast?

JOHN

*B*efore I could shoot, the desert erupted in a ground-shaking explosion.

I'd never experienced an earthquake, but if it was

anything like this, I was definitely going to avoid them in the future.

The blast knocked me to the ground as dust clouds eclipsed the sun.

I hunkered down and waited.

As the sky finally cleared, I got to my feet—battered and covered in sand. I looked in both directions, trying to get my bearings.

My nemesis must have set up some kind of kill zone in the desert, timed to explode when the convoy drove through. An elementary technique—it was a trick I'd used myself dozens of times.

Even though I had attacked the agent, his system appeared to have been programmed to operate on its own.

The only problem was . . .

The convoy—alerted by our fighting—was now speeding away in the distance.

Damn, I was pissed. This had really ruined my day.

I had no idea who'd been out here getting in my way. I didn't even have a clue as to whether the agent was dead or alive.

But either way, I was determined to learn his name. I swore that when I found out, if he wasn't dead already—he was sure as hell going to wish he was.

I started to walk away. But then I spotted something—a light blinking on and off in the rubble from the mine-shack explosion.

A laptop computer. Unbelievable. It was still working.

I grinned and ran to retrieve it.

JANE

Goddamn bastard.

I hadn't expected a difficult mission. And I sure as hell hadn't expected any unidentified players. My team was thorough, organized, and always well prepared. We were better than this. But this pie-eating punk had made us look like amateurs.

I didn't even want to think about what Father would say about tonight's miserable failure.

But one thing I swore as I rendezvoused with my team: I would learn this man's name.

And then I would make him sorry he'd ever met me.

JOHN

Back in the city I stopped by the diner to tell Eddie what I'd found.

I stared into a mug of black coffee as Eddie wolfed down the Hungry Man Breakfast Special. Day or night, that guy could pack it away.

But I wasn't hungry. All I could think about was my ruined assignment and the agent who had thrown me off my game.

I fingered my nicked ear. It had been a long time since anybody had come quite that close to putting a bullet through my brain. "Two hitters. You ever have two hitters on the same square?"

"Not that I'm aware of," Eddie said around a mouthful of eggs and toast. "You get a good look at him?"

As if the situation wasn't weird enough, something about my opponent kept gnawing at me, too. I shrugged, trying to remember. "Little thing. Buck ten, buck fifteen tops . . ." *Not much bigger than Jane,* I thought. That's when it hit me. "I'm not so sure it was a *him.*"

Eddie's fork clattered to his plate. He just stared at me. "You got beat up by a *girl*?"

Ouch. I didn't care for the way he'd phrased that. "I think so," I admitted.

I swiveled on my stool to face him. "Eddie, she was a *pro.*"

Eddie shrugged and went back to vacuuming his plate. "Well, then, this should be easy. I mean, how many hitters are chicks, right?"

He had a point. Hell, that would eliminate most operatives in the whole goddamn business.

Eddie's eyes drifted after the waitress. "I'd like to see *her* kick my ass . . ." Eddie's appetite for women was almost as voracious as his appetite for ham and eggs. I waited patiently for him to remember I was there.

"You got anything to go on?" he said, turning back to me at last.

I did—the laptop I'd found in the rubble. It was pretty beat-up, but it was still alive. And I knew a girl who could do wonders with twisted bits of metal.

I gulped down my coffee and spun off the stool. "See you later, Eddie."

I slipped into the back room of my favorite digital chop shop and looked around for a whiz kid named Gwen.

I spotted her bent over a worktable covered with junk—it looked like a computer graveyard. With her spiked hair and White Stripes tank top, she looked more like a baby-sitter than the electronics genius I knew her to be.

I told her I had a slightly damaged laptop, then laid the machine on the counter for her to examine.

She surveyed the charred wreckage the laptop had become. "You put a campfire out with it?" she asked skeptically.

I smiled. *Very funny.*

"My advice to you?" she said, wiping her hands on a rag.

I leaned forward hopefully.

"Buy a new one."

"This one has sentimental value for its owner," I insisted.

"Who's that?"

I smiled innocently. "I was hoping you could tell me."

Gwen chewed her lip and examined the machine. "No serials," she pointed out. "Looks like it's government or something." She threw up her hands. "It's untraceable."

Okay. It wasn't hard to tell where this was going. But I waited, the ball in her court.

"There *is* something we *might* do. It wouldn't be easy"—she glanced up at me—"or legal."

I forked over a portrait of Ben Franklin, my favorite president.

"Oh," she said, in a voice like Shirley Temple, "it'd be *twice* as illegal as that."

Of course it would. I held out Franklin's twin.

She grinned and snatched it from my fingers, then went to work.

Of course, there was no way I was letting that precious bit of evidence out of my sight, so I hung around, staring out the window. Thinking about all that had happened.

"So why you gotta know so bad anyway?" Gwen asked as she attacked the guts of the machine.

"You know me, Gwen. Just an honest citizen trying to return some lost property . . ."

"Yeah, right."

". . . who's given you two hundred bucks to shut up and get on with it."

She just laughed and kept digging.

At last she let out a tiny whoop. "Here we go. Upgraded RAM module." She bipped the bar code on her reader. Information flooded the screen of her diagnostic machine.

"Okay," Gwen said, scanning the news. "The chip's Chinese, imported by Dynamix, retailed by blah blah blah . . ." She started typing, her fingers a blur. "I think I can get you a billing address." She glanced sideways at me. "You're just sending flowers, right?"

"Chocolate," I murmured in my sexiest voice.

"Stop, you're getting me hot." Her fingers flew over the keyboard.

I was about to make another joke when she stopped, and read, then shook her head. "No name, just an address."

"Fine," I said eagerly. "Let me have it."

"Card's registered to Five-fifty Lexington, fifty-second floor."

An electric shock shot through me, a jolt that had nothing to do with anything in Gwen's shop.

The address sounded familiar. Too familiar.

Gwen peered at me. "You know this place?"

I shook my head. Unsure.

And something in my gut told me: I would regret finding out.

JANE

$\mathcal{I}$ stormed into the Triple-Click project room, breathing fire.

Thank God John was "out of town" and I was supposedly spending the night at my parents' house. I was furious, and I knew I would have had a damned hard time playing the perfect little wife around him right now.

Not that he would have noticed.

But I was thankful I had nothing else to think about but my job.

I slammed my briefcase down on my desk. "We lost the package," I announced. "The FBI secured him this morning."

Jasmine sank back in her chair. She knew as well as I did that this was a big deal.

Bottom line: We'd fucked up.

But I am notorious for being a damn sore loser. I absolutely have to win. And I wasn't through with my little interfering mischief maker.

Bottom line: The dude was gonna pay.

"I want to know who that bastard is and what he was doing on my patch—"

"Jane . . ."

"—let's see the tape," I rushed on. "If the tunnel entrance has a traffic camera, we can hack into—"

"Jane . . ."

"—and I want to talk to—"

"*Jane!*"

I turned, scowling with impatience. Jessie was holding out a phone.

Shit. If Jessie was interrupting my war dance, then there could be only one person on the other end of that phone.

Jessie shrugged. "*Father.*"

We shared a dark glance. She knew I'd rather face a firing squad than take that call. But courage is part of my job description, so I didn't hesitate. I took the phone and said hello.

Ouch. Father's formal accent sliced through me like an ice pick when he was angry. I listened without interrupting, knowing I deserved every blistering word.

Still, I tried to stick up for my team. "The FBI secured the package. The window's closed..." I flinched at Father's response. "Sir, there was another player—"

"I *told* you we couldn't afford any mistakes on this end."

For some strange reason, a chill ran through me. I quickly shook it off like water on a wet dog. "But there was another player at the—"

"We do *not* leave witnesses," Father interrupted. "Zero exposure. If this player ID'd you—"

"I understand, sir."

"You know the rules," Father went on, his voice cold as ice. "You've got forty-eight hours. Clean the scene, Jane."

I held my breath as he paused; he seemed about to say something else . . .

But then the line went dead.

Yeah, nice talking to you, too, Dad.

But I knew the rules. And I'd been in the business long enough to know that Father meant what he said and said what he meant. There would be no second chances.

Success was the only option.

But that was okay. Succeeding was one of my favorite things to do.

I slammed down the phone and turned to my crew.

I was still angry, yes, but also exhilarated by the

adrenaline pumping into my veins, the thrill of a new chase. "We've got a new target," I informed them. "Let's find out who he is."

JOHN

Lexington Avenue. I checked the address again. Two more blocks. Two more blocks till I knew.

I didn't know whether to run or drag my heels. So I walked, with my hands stuffed in my pockets, head down.

Two crosswalks later I knew I could no longer put off the inevitable. So I steeled myself and looked up. There it was: 550 Lexington Avenue. A typical up-scale skyscraper.

As I walked the last few yards, my pace quickened, and I shoved through the revolving door into the lobby, nearly sprinted to the building register on the wall as I dug the crumpled paper out of my pocket to double-check an address I knew by heart.

There. Suite 5204E. And beside it, a company name. TRIPLE-CLICK, COMPUTER TEMP AGENCY.

The blood drained from my face. "Not possible . . ." I muttered under my breath.

I felt as if that desert explosion was knocking me off my feet all over again.

Did I know the company? Hell, yeah, I did. In fact, I knew someone who worked there.

Knew her well.

Or maybe . . . maybe not at all.

Someone who just happened to be a very close relation of mine . . .

JANE

We taped our missions, whenever possible. (Although I'd specifically "forgotten" to have the crew record my night with Marco Racin—some memories just shouldn't be preserved for posterity.) You never knew when some casual visual detail might reveal some major information.

So I ran the tape of our botched operation in slow motion, examining every square inch of the screen. When I got to the tape of my Buggy Dude, I zoomed in, hoping to see what perhaps I'd missed before.

Something shiny caught my eye. I leaned forward.

It looked like . . .

I blinked.

It looked like a hip flask, the kind you'd use to carry your preferred brand of booze to the Kentucky Derby, or some other posh event. Like bourbon.

Or scotch . . .

I started to move on, but something made me take a closer look.

The flask looked familiar, which totally freaked me out. It was like checking into a new hotel room—and finding one of your possessions in an empty drawer.

Of course, a lot of men carried flasks. I bet at least 50, 60 percent of them were silver, too. Maybe more.

I advanced the tape a little and noticed something else, lying on the ground at the man's feet.

Pie.

So what? I made a pie just the other day. Key lime pie, as a matter of fact. John's favorite. I'd even packed him a lunch with a slice of that pie the night before he told me he had to go out of town.

Did he take it with him? *I don't know—I didn't check the fridge.*

But hey, lots of people made pie every day. You could get it at any deli or supermarket. All kinds.

Nothing special about pie.

So what if the pie in this video looked like key lime, too. And I'm sure lots of women knew how to make that special distinctive crimp in the edge of the crust. The one I thought I made up. My signature, kind of.

Really, a guy carrying a silver flask and eating pie, even key lime pie, pie with a special signature crimp to the crust, well, what was so unusual . . .

Quickly I rewound to the man's face and blew it up to life size. The image was still blurry, impossible to see clearly—plus my subject was wearing a helmet and goggles.

He could be anybody. Really.

But the tilt to his head, the set to his shoulders . . . the attitude in the way he stood . . .

I'd seen this man before.

I couldn't get a clear view of his eyes because of the goggles. The helmet hid everything else but his mouth.

I stared at that mouth. Those lips . . .

Holy shit.

I felt the blood rush to my face, and I swallowed hard as I leaned closer, so close my nose almost touched the screen. So close my lips were almost touching those lips . . .

"It's your husband," Jasmine said behind me.

I choked and spun around.

But Jasmine wasn't looking at the face on the screen. She was holding out the phone.

"It's your husband," she repeated. "He's back from Atlanta. Wants to know about dinner."

He was back. From Atlanta. Or wherever the hell he'd really been.

Like maybe somewhere even hotter.

Sandier . . .

The floor seemed to tilt. Images of life and work collided into conclusions that made no sense.

Your husband ...

Familiar words that suddenly had no meaning.

"Tell him ..." My voice faltered. Tell him what?

That I know everything?

I know nothing.

Not anymore.

"Tell him ..."

Jasmine peered curiously at me.

"Tell him ... dinner's at seven."

I turned around in my chair to stare once more at those lips. Lips that could send a woman reeling.

Or whisper a lifetime of pretty lies.

JOHN

Dinner's at seven? That's all she can say? *Dinner's at seven?!*

"It always is," I muttered into the phone, then hung up.

I wandered back out onto the sidewalk and stood for a minute, gazing up to the fifty-second floor.

Dinner's at seven, dinner's at seven . . . Jesus Christ! I'd been setting my watch by *dinner's at seven* for five goddamn years. I'd been brushing my teeth beside her, sharing closet space with her, hell—I'd been sleeping next to her, completely un-armed and totally exposed, for what seemed like centuries! And all this time . . .

She'd been slipping out to assassinate people when I wasn't looking.

Christ Almighty! Yesterday she tried to fucking

kill my ass—and all she can say is, "Dinner's at seven?!"

I'd played mind games with some of the most devious operatives in the business.

But this woman—God, she was gonna blow my mind.

I leaned on a corner trash can like a drunk about to hurl, and slowly dropped the crumpled address into the garbage.

Get a grip, I told myself.

I was a pro. I'd been trained to function in even the most dangerous situations. I had the experience and the skills to deal with this, too.

That's when anger overtook the shock, adrenaline goading me to take action.

I stood up, straightened my cuffs, and strode purposefully toward the parking garage, where I'd left my car.

I had a dangerous mission to complete.

I was heading home for dinner.

JANE

J left the office early for once. Told Jasmine I wasn't feeling well. Said maybe I'd picked up a bug in the desert. Which made me wonder . . .

Note to self: Check car, house, person for any other kind of bug that hitter might have planted while trying to break my neck.

Jasmine accepted my excuse without question. At least not spoken. Her eyes asked me everything.

But I couldn't talk about my suspicions yet. Couldn't tell anyone—not even Jasmine, who knew almost everything about me.

I just wasn't ready.

I had to be sure, see for myself, that my life with John was a total optical illusion.

By the time I got home, my hands ached from gripping the steering wheel so hard. Only one thing had kept me from losing it.

Dinner's at seven.

On the drive home I planned the menu in detail. Decided which china and table linens to use. Debated whether to stop for flowers.

I wanted—*needed*—everything to be perfect. One last time.

Before everything fell apart.

JOHN

My headlights flashed across the house, the yard, the driveway, the garage. Things I never really looked at anymore, they were so familiar.

Suddenly my perfect home in the burbs looked like the set for a TV show called *Somebody Else's Life*.

I killed the lights and stared at the house for a minute, with just one question on my mind.

What the hell was I getting for dinner *tonight*?

When she tried to kill me on that mountain, had she really been trying to kill *me*? Her husband? Or was I simply an enemy operative who'd gotten in the way of her hit?

Did *she* know about *me*? And did she know I knew about *her*?

Jesus. Could two people really live together in a house with secrets like ours, and have no idea what was going on?

I looked at the kitchen window.

No sign of my darling wife.

Was she making dinner? Or cooking up plans for a murder?

With fear and loathing, I forced my wedding band on my finger and made myself open the car door.

The hinge screeched. A dog barked in the distance. Shrubbery rustled by the front door.

Tonight my lovely house looked incredibly menacing in the shadows, like a beautiful woman with evil on her mind.

On full alert, I walked up the sidewalk and opened the front door. *Lucy, I'm home . . .*

Cautiously I stepped into the front hall, one hand on my suitcase, one hand in my pocket where I kept my courage.

I'm talking about my gun. Not the booze.

I eased the door closed and moved forward, eyes darting everywhere . . .

"Perfect timing."

I jumped and almost shot my foot off.

Jane—she'd appeared out of nowhere, silent and deadly. Dressed to kill, you might say. And holding up two chilled martinis.

The perfect wife. Just like old times. As if the entire universe hadn't changed since I went away.

I nodded at the martinis. "This is a surprise." She bitched at me all the time about my drinking.

"A pleasant one, I hope," she said with a flirtatious smile. She thrust the fragile glass toward me, and by reflex, I took it. With my gun hand.

Coincidence? Or the clever strategy of an experienced assassin?

Then she leaned in for a kiss.

I didn't close my eyes.

So I noticed—neither did she.

"You're back early," she said. *A challenge.*

"I missed you."

"Missed you, *too,*" she replied.

Was it my imagination? Or did her eyes dart to my bandaged ear?

But she'd turned away, motioning toward the dining room. "Shall we?"

"After you," I said, the perfect gentleman. Perfectly careful.

With a casual shrug, she turned and led the way. I let my eyes roam up and down her swaying curves, inspecting her for clues, weapons . . . really looking at her for the first time in years.

Let me tell you, that outfit revealed a lot more than it concealed. Definitely no weapons on board. At least not the conventional kind.

I might have enjoyed the view if I hadn't been so damned worried she was about to blow my head off.

When I entered the dining room, my apprehension jacked up a notch. The joint was all decked out like we were expecting the royal family for dinner—flowers, the best linens. More than one fork.

Watch your ass, I warned myself. *The bitch is definitely up to something.*

"Thought you only broke these out for special occasions," I said.

"Isn't dinner with my husband special enough?" she said.

She even held out my goddamn chair for me.

I sat down slowly, my eyes never leaving hers, all senses on alert. Like a maître d' in a fancy restaurant, she removed my white linen napkin, and I must admit I flinched when she whip-cracked it open before laying it across my lap.

"Why, thank you," I said, playing along.

"Anything for you," she cooed.

Yeah, I bet.

As she walked around behind me, I surreptitiously slid my knife into my lap, hiding it under the napkin.

She didn't seem to notice but just skipped out through the kitchen door, tossing a coy smile over her shoulder as she disappeared.

I nearly laughed out loud and reached for my cocktail.

Till I saw something through the swinging kitchen door. A can of Drano sitting out on the counter.

I froze with my martini inches from my lips.

Jeez. What the hell did Drano smell like? I sniffed my drink. It smelled okay. I thought. Maybe . . . But that didn't prove anything.

Keeping my eye on the closed kitchen door, I quickly dumped my drink into a vase of flowers in the center of the table, hoping they wouldn't explode.

As I waited, I studied the table, looking for . . . I wasn't sure what: clues, weapons, traps. Every piece of cutlery flickered menacingly in the candlelight. The wine became a vehicle for poison; the table runner a strangulation device. The centerpiece, a place to conceal a deadly grenade.

Then my little wife was back, smiling like *Playboy* meets *Good Housekeeping* over a steaming roast.

A roast that had a wicked-looking knife sticking out of its back.

"Mmm. Pot roast. My favorite."

The knife glinted in the candlelight as Jane sharpened it, wielding it as if a roast weren't the only thing she knew how to carve.

Shit. My hand shot out and clamped down on her wrist. "No, no, no," I murmured. "You've been on your feet in the kitchen. Allow me."

For a moment I felt her resist, but I lovingly disarmed her. I noticed she quickly stepped away from me, now that the razor-sharp blade was in my hand.

As I held the knife, ready to slice into the meat, I kept an eye on her reflection in the shining blade.

Fuck! She'd pulled an even larger knife from that frilly little apron of hers. How the hell did she smuggle that in? The thing was big enough to hack a path through the jungle, but she was using it to cut our baked potatoes in half. Like it was what she always used.

Like Martha Stewart gone mad.

It was crazy. We just stood there, side by side like newlyweds, while maybe plotting how to slash each other's throat. I studied her, watched how easily she handled a knife. Hell, how had I missed this before? This lady had the hands of a master slasher.

I wondered what she'd used for practice.

"How's work?" I asked casually.

"Fine," she replied. Then a funny look crossed her face. "Actually, we had a little problem with a commission this week."

"Yeah?" I asked, instantly alert.

"Mm-hmm. A double booking with another firm."

I placed a perfectly carved slice of pot roast onto Jane's plate. "Everything work out okay?"

She slid a potato onto mine, the blade a little too close to a similar-shaped piece of my anatomy that she might not be so averse to slicing. "Not yet," she said. "But it will."

Okay, up till now, you could have argued that I

was being paranoid, that I was reading too much into every little thing. But now I was definitely getting the sense that we were talking in riddles and code.

We sat down at opposite ends of the table, out of arm's reach. She sipped her wine and waited for me to begin.

I stared down into my plate, hesitating. What if the food was poisoned?

Then I caught Jane watching me carefully. Hell, I couldn't let her know she had me spooked, so I hacked off a hunk of meat like a medieval warrior and boldly took a bite.

"Mmm. This is great," I said, fighting the urge to spit it out on the floor. "You do something new?"

She glared at me for the first time that night. "You *always* ask that."

Yeah, well, what else was I supposed to say after eighteen hundred meals? I chuckled to cover my ass. "I always forget how good it is."

Her smile returned; I cut more meat slowly, playing for time. "Could you pass the—"

Wham! Something skidded across the table, and my hand shot out to catch it.

The salt.

If it had been a blade, I'd have been dead before the smile touched her lips.

In some ways, she was doing what she always did. She always set a nice table, served a nice meal that looked like something out of a magazine. Always strived for pure perfection.

Hell, it was like eating in the same damn restaurant night after night after night.

But tonight she was different. We weren't just in

a different restaurant. We were in a different restaurant on a different planet.

There was an underlying edge to everything. Something subtly different to her moves.

I watched her closely as she reached toward her glass of water. Her movements seemed confident, deliberate; every move a clean straight line.

How had I missed the hard muscles that rippled along her lovely arms? How she moved with the grace of a trained ninja? How alert she was, and how quickly she reacted to every sound?

Like a true professional, conscious of every move, someone who knew that well-conditioned reflexes and decisive moves could sometimes mean the difference between life and death.

Had she been hiding this side of herself? Or had I simply been too bored, too preoccupied, too *stupid* to see what was right here under my nose all along?

"How was Atlanta?" she asked pointedly.

Especially since she knew damn well I hadn't been there.

"Had a problem with some figures," I said easily. "Something didn't add up."

"Big deal?" she asked.

"Life or death."

Our eyes locked across the table. I could see flames—candlelight—flickering in her eyes.

"More wine, dear?" I asked. Before she could even answer, I insisted, "Allow me. It *is* in the middle of the table, after all."

I rose and strode toward her.

And smiled at the fear that leaped in her eyes.

JANE

Look at him.

Goddamn bastard.

Sitting across from me at the table like he's done every night for six long years. Going through the motions like some Toys "Я" Us husband on Everready batteries. Always smiling. Smiling at me. Smiling at everything I said. Smiling at the goddamn pot roast. Without ever really seeing any of it.

While lying to me about everything.

How was your trip to Atlanta, dear?

Oh, fine. A few problems with some figures. Blah blah blah. Except I wasn't even in Atlanta, darling. I was in the desert trying to blow you up with my great big GUNS!

And all the time drinking from the silver flask I'd given him and . . . and . . . *eating my pie!*

I watched him going about the motions. Did he think of me when he was gone? Did he laugh about his stupid little wife as he stuffed my pie into his big fat mouth? Had he joked about what a fool I was while he lay in the arms of some femme fatale operative in postmission bliss?

No wonder he rolled over and went to sleep every night he crawled into bed with me. He wasn't boring. He'd just burned up every ounce of energy living his thrilling double life! Somebody else got his James Bond; all I got was Ward Cleaver. *Father Knows Best.* Leftovers!

The only thing he ever kept me up with all night anymore was his snoring.

Damn him.

Now he was coming toward me like he thought he was Cary Grant, ready to pour me another glass of wine.

Suddenly my heart froze. I didn't like that look in his eye. And here was the question. Did he know it was me he almost killed up on that mountain ravine? Was he here to finish the job?

Maybe he didn't know, didn't know I knew. So maybe he was really just going to pour me some wine.

Or maybe he was just tired of his boring little wife and wanted to kill her off so he could run away with some killer named Natasha!

I watched him move toward me, eyes never leaving mine as he so casually palmed the wine bottle on the way.

Mm-hmm. Cary Grant.

Cary Grant, serial killer.

I tensed, eyeing the bottle in his hand. How easily he could swing it around and smash my skull if he wanted to.

My eyes shot to the nearest knife on the table. I held my breath, crossed my legs, and held out my glass.

Just as he leaned down to pour—or kill—he looked startled.

I realized my dress had drifted up a bit, revealing my bandaged knee and the bruises from my fall on the rocks in the desert.

He let the bottle slip from his grasp.

My hand shot out and caught it in midair. A brilliant save; excellent reflexes.

Not the reflexes of a housewife.

Stupid me.

A slow smile spread across John's face.

Our eyes locked once more.

He knew. And he knew I knew. And now I knew that he knew I knew.

Ah, yes. All of a sudden we were a very knowing couple.

I let the bottle drop.

As it fell in what seemed like slow motion, toward our perfect white carpet, memories flooded my mind—

How we had been in Bogotá. How he always seemed to be in the middle of things. I never questioned why he was there, or why he kept such strange hours for a man overseeing a construction project. All I cared about were those blissful hours he was free to spend in my bed.

When I wasn't making love to him, I'd been out handling my work assignments. Three assassinations in one week.

And the whole time? He must have been doing the same.

The bastard had been lying to me from day one.

With a thud, the wine spilled across the floor, covering the perfect rug with a horrible bloodred stain.

JOHN

We spoke at the same time.

"I'll get a towel," Jane said.

"I'll get it," I said.

An excuse. We both fled.

I ran into my den and shut the door behind me, panting, my mind racing in a million different directions.

In a single night, in a single moment, the whole fucking world had changed. No words spoken. No shots fired.

But our eyes had confessed everything.

She knew; I knew. There was no going back.

Staring into her eyes as the wine spilled, I'd had a flashback. Memories of Bogotá.

I'd never asked her why she was there, hadn't questioned how easily she'd fallen into my bed. I was just so damn glad to have her there. And in between making love, when I'd slipped off to take care of a few assassinations—four in one week—she'd been slipping off to do the same.

The bitch had been lying to me since day one.

She'd tried to kill me before. Now that she knew I knew everything, she really needed me dead.

A door slammed somewhere in the house, and I stopped cold. I pressed my ear to my door, but I heard nothing more. Crossing to my desk, I pulled open the main drawer and tapped open a hidden compartment.

A gun, a clip, and a silencer.

In three quick moves, the parts clicked into place. Then I took a deep breath and stepped out into the hall, the gun behind my back.

I scanned the dining room. The candles flickered ominously. Had she just hurried past them?

"Jane?" I called out. "Honey . . . ?"

No response.

Maybe she didn't answer to that name anymore.

Then I heard a noise outside. My eyes snapped to the window.

The garage door was opening. The car—she was going to drive away!

I raced through the house, out the front door, across the lawn, just as she began to back out of the garage. I lunged into the driveway and blocked her path.

"STOP THE CAR, JANE!"

Instead, she hit the gas, rammed our beautiful Mercedes-Benz wagon over the low wall, and tore across the grass.

I knew there was no way I could catch her if I just followed her. But maybe I could cut through the neighbors' backyards . . .

Dumb idea. Especially in the dark. The Colemans' yard was easy, but then I leaped some bushes, and—

Damn. Landed on some kind of kiddie play set. Once

I fought my way out of the swings, I ran right into a yard with a barking dog . . .

Let's just say I got up close and personal with just about every kind of outdoor suburban paraphernalia imaginable before I made it to the end of my run.

Might have been funny, if it was a movie.

Finally I made it to the end of the block and climbed a fence—just as Jane's car careened around the corner.

Gotta admire a girl who can drive on two wheels.

Our eyes locked.

"Something you want to tell me, hon?" I shouted.

The look she gave me could have set a snowman on fire, and maybe that's why the fence chose that moment to collapse. Down I went, plunging headfirst into a muddy puddle. Which would have been bad enough. But then—

Bang! The impact caused me to accidentally fire my gun.

"Oh, shit!"

One thing about a bullet: You can't take it back. It's kind of like sex, you know? Once that hammer slams down and says *Go, baby!* it's a done deal.

And "accidentally" is never a good thing.

But you know what's even worse than accidentally shooting off your gun?

When that shot chooses—out of all the targets in the universe—to slam through your wife's windshield. Oh, shit. If I didn't just kill her . . . she was going to kill me.

JANE

Maybe John wanted to hang around the house and play cops and robbers. Cowboys and Indians. Spy vs. spy.

But I was sick of games. And I couldn't bear to be in that house with him one more minute. So I ran.

"Six years," I muttered as I backed out of the garage and stomped on the gas. "Six years!"

I sped down the street and swerved around a corner. Then suddenly my headlights hit John like a spotlight: He was hanging at the top of a fence looking like a convict making a break for it. He must have cut through our neighbors' backyards.

I glared at him as he shouted some lame taunt that I couldn't understand. Then the fence he was clinging to fell over, tossing him into the mud, and the next thing I knew—

A bullet slammed through my windshield!

I couldn't believe it. The bastard was trying to kill me!

I instinctively closed my eyes and slammed on the brakes as I braced myself for impact.

It took a moment to realize the bullet had narrowly missed my head.

Gasping in relief, I stared out the window, through the bullet hole, at my assassin.

Otherwise known as my husband.

"You bastard!" I shouted.

John got to his feet, covered in mud. "Okay, honey, stay calm," he called out as he ran toward me like a madman, waving his hands—and gun. "You know I didn't mean to—"

But I was too angry to think straight. All I knew was that I didn't want to hear any more of his lies.

I aimed the car at his belt buckle—and burned rubber.

"That's it!" he shouted. "Overreact."

But then he realized I wasn't kidding.

"JANE!" he shouted. "STOP THE CAR!"

"Sorry, baby!" I muttered under my breath. "You can't tell me what to do anymore."

One of the many things John didn't know about me was that I'd played myriad forms of chicken over the years in my job, and I never lost. There are countless bad guys who'd be glad to swear to that fact, but they're all dead.

Wham! At the last second John leaped onto my car and vaulted over the roof.

I quickly glanced back to see where he'd landed. Okay, maybe I looked to make sure he was okay.

But there was no sign of him.

Which could only mean . . .

HE WAS ON THE ROOF!

Half a second later, a side rear window exploded as John kicked through it and landed in the backseat covered in shattered glass.

A ballsy move, I had to admit.

"Now, *look*—" John began as he leaned forward from the backseat.

But I was already making my own ballsy move: I popped my door and leaped out of the car, barrel-rolling across the street into a soft, overgrown yard.

Dear John, I wanted to tell him as I landed, *good-bye. Our marriage is over.*

You can have the car.

But alas, he was screaming too loud to hear.

JOHN

Holy shit!
She jumped out of the fucking car—with me in the backseat!

Uh-huh. *Definitely* mad about the bullet!

I stared out the back window. Saw her stand up and brush herself off like it was nothing.

And felt the car—*wham!*—hit the curb.

"JANE!" I shouted as the car caught air. "We need to *taaaaaaalk*!"

Somehow, later that evening, I found myself on Eddie's doorstep again—wet, muddy, bruised—but in one piece.

At least my body was.

I wasn't sure about my heart or my mind. The first was bashed, and the second I was about to lose.

It was late, but I needed a friend. And not someone who was just a barbecue buddy like Martin Coleman.

The door cracked open and Eddie peeked out. Then the door swung wide. "What the hell happened to you?" he gasped.

I limped over the threshold. "My wife."

JANE

Not knowing where else to go, I headed for my safe house—the Triple-Click project room. It was late, but Jasmine was still there.

She took one look at me and shoved me into a comfortable chair.

I took a deep breath—and told her my news.

"Say that again?"

I glared at her. It was hard enough to get the words out once. Besides, she'd heard me the first time.

The operative we'd been ordered to kill—the man who'd tried to kill *me*—was a known entity. Relatively speaking.

My husband.

"But that's just so implausible," Jasmine said as she sank down into a chair. "What are the odds?" She shook her head. "But it could be worse, Jane."

The scowl I shot her could have sharpened a Cuisinart blade. "Really?"

Jasmine shrugged comically, and I would have laughed if the circumstances hadn't been so dismal. We were two girlfriends sharing the sordid details of a husband's infidelities. Only in my case the betrayal went far beyond an affair with a neighbor or a lap dance gone awry on a business trip.

If only I didn't know, injured wife might say to sympathetic friend. *If only I could pretend it didn't happen . . .*

But I'm not an ordinary woman, nor is my life an ordinary life. Two roads diverged many years ago when I had chosen the road less traveled. I'd made peace with who I was.

Then John had stumbled into my life and complicated everything. Made me feel things I'd never known I could feel for anyone. Made me long for a life I should've known I could never have. In the heat of the moment, I had let the danger and romance of Bogotá overpower me, and I'd let the enemy capture the one thing I had sworn never to give up.

My heart.

Jasmine had warned me, but I'd refused to listen.

Lucky for me my best friend was a hard-ass intelligence professional who had a lot more to offer than a hankie and a slice of coffee cake.

"Okay. It's a little awkward, I admit," Jasmine said. "But face it. He's a man. They should all come with an expiration date." There was a look in Jasmine's eyes, a look that said she was speaking from experience. Painful experience. And for the first time I wondered about her life outside of work. It was something we didn't talk about much in the offices of Triple-Click.

I fiddled with my wedding ring.

"Look," Jasmine said. "There is an upside . . . You don't love him. You'll kill him. Nobody does that better than you."

I didn't respond.

I could feel Jasmine staring at me, trying to read my thoughts.

"Wait a minute," she said. "Don't tell me you're actually in love with him . . ."

The blistering look I shot her was enough to send even her away. She was an experienced operative who knew how to dodge friendly fire.

Ah, hell. I'd apologize tomorrow, but for now, I was glad to be alone.

I hit the office fridge, bringing back a tumbler of ice and a bottle of pricey scotch.

I filled up my glass like it was Diet Coke, then clutched the drink between both hands and shotgunned it. Not the most elegant way to drink the stuff. But it did the trick.

This was—after all—a special occasion.

I refilled my glass, then slid the wedding ring from my finger and stared at my naked hand. A pale ghost of a ring remained on my skin where the band had protected the flesh all these years from the harsh realities of daily life.

Would the mark fade? Or was it a scar I'd have to live with for years to come?

Don't tell me you're actually in love with him . . .

Jasmine's question hung in the air.

God help me, I was afraid of what my real answer might be.

But I was at a fork in the road again, and I could only travel down one path.

Really, there was only one way to go.

I dropped the ring to the floor. Took another drink. Then did what I could admit to no one: I, Jane Smith—trained assassin, coldhearted professional killer—dropped my head in my hands and wept.

JOHN

Eddie may be slow in some departments. But that night he gave me instant advice.

After I poured out all the sorry details, he lit into me with a bunch of *I told you sos.* (Okay. I deserved 'em.) Then he laid it on the line.

"Take her out."

I stood in his doorway, all riled up, and knew as soon as he said it that it was the only way. "You're right, you're absolutely right, I'm gonna take her out." I punched the air for emphasis.

"Now you're talking," Eddie said. "I like where your head's at, brother."

I reached past the cookie jar, the near-rancid chunk of cheddar cheese, and the open jar of mustard with the knife still sticking out of it and grabbed a handy machine gun that was lying on his kitchen counter. For once, I was glad Eddie was such a slob. "I'm gonna borrow this, okay?"

Eddie nodded as casually as if I'd asked to bum a cigarette. I grabbed the gun, and pumped up on adrenaline, I stormed out the door.

Macho commando dude on a mission . . . to kill his wife.

But somewhere out in the cool night air, something said, *Hang on to your ammo, dude.*

Maybe it was the stars. Maybe it was the schizophrenic voices inside my head.

Whatever it was, I couldn't make myself walk out of

the yard. I just stood there, like I was trapped by some kind of psychological electric dog fence.

I was tired. Yeah, that was it.

With a sigh, I walked back to the house and stepped inside. "It's four in the morning," I explained to Eddie. "Tomorrow I'll get her."

"Yeah, yeah," Eddie agreed, "kill her tomorrow. It's late." He took the gun from my hands. "You want to crash here?"

I started to say, *No, I'll head on home.*

But then I realized—I didn't have one.

So I took Eddie up on his offer.

Suddenly overwhelmed with physical and mental exhaustion, I curled up on Eddie's ratty little couch—which was about the size of Baby Bear's bed. Eddie scrounged up a blanket for me and covered me up. It was a little kid's blanket, embroidered with kittens and rainbows. I guess it must have been his baby blanket or something, because at first he didn't seem to want to let go of it.

"Good night, Eddie," I said, fading fast.

"'Night, John," he said. He let go of the blanket then and turned out the light.

I lay there, struggling to get comfortable. The blanket only covered about half of me. Then I felt something lumpy under my head.

I snuck my hand under the pillow and rooted around. At last I pulled out a .45 automatic wedged down under the cushions. That Eddie . . . like my mom used to say, he'd lose his head if it wasn't attached. Yawning, I let it drop to the floor, then tried to forget everything by going to sleep.

Tomorrow, I promised myself. *Tomorrow I'd do her for sure . . .*

JANE

My beautiful home—!

My team was tearing it upside down, and it was all I could do not to scream at them: *Stop! Stop!*

It was the home I'd fantasized about as a young girl. Nice neighborhood. Nice street. Nice yard.

Inside, everything was spacious and lovely. Thick carpet. Matching cups lined up on a shelf. Refrigerator always stocked with your favorite food. And a beautiful bedroom shared with a handsome husband, the man of my dreams.

Everything perfect. Like something out of a magazine.

Now a trained team of agents was tearing it apart, poking through all its secrets.

Julie shouted orders like a drill sergeant. "Pocket litter. Receipts. Matchbooks. You know what to do."

They did, and so did I. How many times had I torn someone's life apart till it was nothing but fingerprints and fibers?

I trained these women, so I knew they were good, and I knew what we were here to do. They were doing serious CSI forensics work. Soon they'd be searching John's e-mail, hunting through our bills, digging through our drawers, our memories, our trash.

As if dissecting things, tearing them apart, would help me understand.

I told myself to get a grip and get the job done. The sooner the better.

As I walked through the living room, I saw Jessie pick up a glass figurine, and I winced. "I'll get that."

I ignored her knowing look and pocketed the trinket. So I'd palmed a tiny souvenir from the old days. Who cared?

See? I could dump a whole box of photos onto the floor, and not even feel compelled to look at them.

But then I sank to my knees. Beneath the pile of photos I

found a yellowed Spanish-language newspaper, a pressed flower slipping from between its pages.

Carefully I picked it up, remembering . . .

Our first morning-after together. The coffee he brought, the newspaper with this pitiful little weedy wildflower tucked inside, an uncomplicated gift of love.

Even a Vulcan would have felt a flicker of nostalgia.

"Find anything?" Jasmine asked.

I glanced up and found her studying me, then I cleared the lump in my throat. "Just checking the personal effects of the target," I said.

I tossed the newspaper on a pile and left the room.

As I drifted through the rooms, watching my crew work, it was as if I were seeing my home for the first time. I remembered how the living room had looked when we first moved in—completely empty, and full of promise. John and I had shared a candlelight dinner of pizza and wine on an upended crate our first night. And later we'd made love on the floor . . .

My heart twisted. I hadn't thought of that in years.

Now the house was completely furnished and beautifully decorated with elegant furniture, beautiful accessories.

When had it stopped feeling wonderful?

I wandered upstairs and stopped at a framed photograph of me and John at Coney Island. Smiling.

Smiling and lying.

I felt someone looking at me and glanced through the doorway to my bedroom.

My big stuffed bear sat on the edge of the bed, saying hello with his goofy grin. It was hard not to grin back, thinking of the day I won him, at the street festival in Little Italy. The look on John's face when I . . .

Then I saw a knife plunge into Bear's heart. I stared in horror as one of my associates sliced him open and began to rummage through his stuffing for some clue. A sob rose in my throat.

But then I lifted my chin. I could *not* do this. My life in this house had been a clever cover, nothing more.

And then I heard John's voice coming from the bedroom.

My God. Was he here? In the middle of all this?

I hurried into the bedroom and found what looked like a sleepover party: A bunch of my coworkers were curled up on my bed watching vacation videos. *My* vacation videos.

A video of Mr. and Mrs. Smith dancing on the beach.

That's where John's voice was coming from. My voice, too. And laughter. Lots of laughter.

"What *is* this?" I demanded.

"Looks like your honeymoon," Janet said.

"I know what it is!" I snapped. "What are you doing with it?"

"Research," Jade said defensively. "Background. On the target." The other girls nodded.

Bloody hell! I had just discovered that my entire marriage was a lie and that my husband was a stranger; I didn't want to watch my goddamn honeymoon video!

"I've never seen you look so happy," Janet said with a sigh.

Goddammit! I didn't want to see videos of me happy in John's arms! I didn't want to remember how perfect it felt. I had thought my old life was a faded memory. But now I knew it was even worse.

It had all been a total lie.

Even our honeymoon . . .

Flames of anger devoured what was left of my heart.

Yet I was as cold as ice. "Okay, ladies," I said briskly, "this room's wrapped."

Reluctantly they filed out of the bedroom. My bedroom. I reached for the remote to stop the video and turn off the TV . . .

But I couldn't help myself. It was like driving by a car wreck. I knew I shouldn't, but out of morbid curiosity, I looked.

Oh, God. John and me . . . in an island paradise. Laughing,

kissing, fooling around. As if life were as beautiful and sunny as the sky above us.

I barely recognized myself. Had I ever really been that happy?

No, I told myself. *It was only a dream. A beautiful, delicious . . . lie-infested dream.*

I hit the remote, and the memories disappeared as easily as if I'd shut off a Disney video. You know, *Cinderella,* or one of those other deluded-girl movies.

I walked to the TV, ejected the tape, and filed it where it belonged.

In the trash.

After that, I made an executive decision to leave the rest of the job inside to my crew. I'd gone in, faced it, and filed it.

With one final notation: *Jane Smith doesn't live here anymore.*

Outside, I had one more project to handle.

The toolshed.

My domain had always been the kitchen—hell, I'd learned to cook out of necessity. During my childhood, it was cook for myself or don't eat—and so I tackled cooking with the same obsession with perfection I'd applied to everything else. I'd become a goddamn gourmet, if I did say so myself.

But the toolshed was all John's. I never cared what he stored there or why he went in. Which, now that I thought about it, was pretty damn often.

So I went in hungry, sure I'd struck gold. I flipped a switch, and a hanging bulb glared to life.

What a mess!

I popped open toolboxes, dug through drawers. Hell, I didn't even know what most of this guy junk was. And then . . . I heard something.

Hollow sounds beneath my feet, my footsteps echoing faintly.

I grinned. Fake floor!

I stomped. More echoes.

I'd found the mother lode.

I grabbed a flashlight and went to work.

I guess John never expected anyone to suspect him, at least not here, at home in the burbs.

Yeah, he had it locked up, but nothing heavy duty. I moved aside some kind of bench thing and found a safety box in the floor. Combination locks were one of my specialties, so I made short work of opening it. Next, I found an easy trapdoor handle and I was in.

When I dropped to my feet, I shined the flashlight at the walls.

Holy shit! It was a goddamn arsenal!

The place was lined with weapons of every kind and size. It was a weapons Wal-Mart!

And on the shelves were stacks and stacks of cash. In every denomination. Lots of foreign bills, too. More money than the local bank branch probably ever had in its vaults.

My face broke out in the first genuine smile of the day. Cleaning out the toolshed was not usually my idea of a fun chore. But today, I thought I'd like it just fine.

That's when my girls showed up and were equally amazed.

"Bag it," I told them. "Bag it all."

Like the Grinch who stole Christmas, we quickly packed up all of John's toys and stuffed them up the ladder. Out on the street, I watched in grim satisfaction as my associates loaded a black van with pillowcases and sheets that they'd filled with weapons.

I smiled as two little neighbor girls skipped past.

"What's going on, Mrs. Smith?" one asked me.

"Garden party, girls," I said with a smile.

JOHN

I glanced at my watch.

Time enough to down one for the road.

I pulled my silver hip flask from my pocket, un-screwed the top, and started to knock back a slug.

But then I stopped and read the inscription. It was as if I were reading it for the very first time.

To dodging bullets. Love, Jane.

Damn. A cryptic message from the past.

Had it been fair warning? Had she known, even back then—even as she'd writhed and moaned beneath my touch, even as she'd whispered sweet promises in my ear—that one day the bullets I'd be dodging would be hers?

Hell. Suddenly I lost my taste for top-shelf booze, especially the kind choked down from a silver flask. I jammed the top back on.

I oughta throw the damn thing in the trash.

But I decided to keep it. As a reminder of what a stupid fool I'd been.

I stuffed the keepsake back into my pocket, then headed into the nearest corner bar.

Suddenly I had a taste for a brewski. Something ice-cold. Something cheap, but honest.

JANE

Back in the project room at Triple-Click, the machines hummed like well-tuned Jaguars at a stoplight. And so did I.

"Okay, *target profile* is our priority, ladies. Full workup. Uti-lize all means necessary: phone taps, credit cards. Audio scan civilian frequencies."

"With what, Jane?" Jessie asked.

I held up a tiny microcassette. Everyone gazed at it appreciatively. But as I played it, they realized it wasn't the high-tech gadget it appeared to be.

"Hi, you've reached John and Jane Smith. We're not home right now, but leave a message at the tone . . . Beep."

The gang stared at me, but I ignored them.

"And scan all databases for—"

"For what?" Jasmine blurted out sarcastically. " 'John Smith'?"

I opened my mouth, then shut it. I'm ashamed to admit I felt a slow blush creep up my cheeks.

Damn. Of course—John Smith indeed! I suddenly realized I had absolutely no idea what my husband's *real* name was!

How humiliating, among other things.

The girls looked at me with sympathy.

Which really pissed me off!

"*Find* him," I barked.

Okay, so I was losing my signature cool. But a girl had a right, under the circumstances.

"Um, Jane," Julie interrupted timidly. "I think I found him."

My heart leaped like a leopard who'd spotted his prey. The whole crew turned to Julie.

She blanched.

"Well?" I demanded. *"Where is he?"*

Julie gulped. "Here." She punched the keys on her computer, pulling up one of the many security shots we had in place.

Surveillance cameras focused on the elevator doors as they slid open.

Empty!

Was he hiding inside? I zoomed in for a closer view, looking for a shadow, a cuff sticking out into the camera's view.

Nothing. But wait—something glinted on the elevator floor.

I zoomed in closer.

A tiny gold circle reflecting the elevator lights. A wedding band. And inside the circular promise of love, another promise:

A single bullet.

John's message was loud and clear.

"Heat-sensor breach in the perimeter," Jessie suddenly announced.

On-screen the program flashed a 3-D grid of the heating vents—and the thermal image of a man crawling through them.

My eyes asked the question.

Julie pointed up.

As a group, we looked at the ceiling above our heads, waiting for a sound.

Riiiiiing!

I jumped as my cell phone rang. I snapped it open, still scanning the ceiling. I didn't need caller ID to know who was on the line.

"I thought I told you never to bother me at the office," I answered.

"First and last warning, Jane," John said without preamble. "You need to disappear. *Now.*"

"And why would I want to do that?"

"Because," he said, "I can push the button anywhere, anytime."

I couldn't resist. "Baby, you couldn't find the button with both hands and a map."

A moment of silence.

"John?"

"*Now* ended five seconds ago."

We heard a metallic bounce overhead, and followed the sound, across the ceiling, down the wall, to an air vent . . .

Hell! He wasn't kidding! A tiny grenade tumbled out and rolled across the floor. It looked like a Happy Meal prize—a Barbie grenade. But I knew it wasn't a toy.

Milliseconds from death, there wasn't time for my brain to get a message to my legs to *get the hell out of there*!

"*Bang!* You're dead!" John shouted.

The last words I'd ever hear.

A small popping noise, and a blinding flash lit the room. We scattered, a final impotent struggle.

And then . . .

I realized I wasn't dead.

The grenade spit red smoke and fizzled. It was harmless.

We hoped.

But even if it was, I didn't think John would give me another warning. This thing was going down, one way or another.

My way, if I could help it.

"Evac Plan C!" I shouted to my crew. "MOVE!"

I fell on the computer keyboard and keyed in a command: all hard drives swiped clean.

My staff harvested bulging paper files and stuffed them into a burn bin. Without a moment's grief, Jasmine tossed in an incendiary device and—*whomp!* Bye bye files.

Our myriad evacuation plans numbered far into the alphabet, but almost all specified that not a scrap of paper, not a comma, not a footprint of evidence be left behind.

As I completed computer shutdown, the rest of my crew tackled what appeared to be typical office walls: With a few practiced moves, they popped open secret panels and extracted handheld launchers from their hidden compartments.

Also concealed within were buttons reserved for an eleventh-hour departure: Hands hit buttons, and windows shattered in a series of explosions that blew inward, showering the office floor with icelike chunks of glass.

Next my crew hooked the Kevlar cords attached to their launchers onto anchors in the ceiling. They aimed the launchers out the window, and fired grapple hooks with more Kevlar cables attached to them in the direction of the surrounding buildings.

I listened to the satisfying *thkkk!* as the hooks bit into nearby rooftops. Once the cords were yanked tight, the launchers snapped to the ceiling, creating taut, secure escape lines.

One by one the crew grabbed slide-for-life rigs, clicked them onto the escape line, and without a moment's hesitation jumped from the windows into the night sky—fifty stories above Mother Earth.

It was a beautiful move, well planned, and well executed, in far less time than it takes to describe. I admired my crew's levelheaded competence and efficiency. Damn, my girls had guts.

"Come on, Jane!" Jasmine shouted as I was clearing the last hard drive. I shot her a brisk nod indicating that I was on my way, and she disappeared out the window.

I was alone.

I took a half-second glance around the office as smoke drifted through the shattered room. It had provided some semblance of permanence in my life, this place, and I had loved working here.

But it was time to go.

I bid the old office an affectionate adieu, then grabbed my launcher and fired.

But just as I clicked onto the cord, I thought I heard something.

Turning back, I saw John drop from the ceiling.

He turned, gun raised, and made eye contact with me through the swirling smoke.

He had a clear shot.

See? I reminded myself. In this business, a half second of sentimentality could buy your moment of death.

I glared at John, a dare.

He hesitated.

Just enough time to make my escape. On a heady rush of adrenaline, I leaped out the window.

JOHN

I had a clear shot, but I made the mistake of looking into Jane's steel-gray eyes.

It was not the tepid, bored, averted look of the wife I thought I knew, but a steel-gray challenge instead. Hers were the eyes of an adversary who could arrest you with a single glance.

And for a moment, I felt an overwhelming sense of arousal—and I'm not talking about the kind of juvenile jolt an impersonal Victoria Secret catalog or *Sports Illustrated* swimsuit issue can stir up. It was . . . I don't know . . . it was like my whole mind, not just my body, was suddenly turned on to her: How could I destroy what I had an immediate hot desire to pursue?

When I took a moment to contemplate blowing her head off, those gray eyes sparkled and almost scoffed at me.

Then, as casually as if she were stepping onto an elevator, she fucking threw herself out the window.

Heart pounding, I ran straight to the ledge and saw that she was on a guideline.

I guess the pursuit thing kicked in pretty damn hard at that moment—*hell, if I was letting this babe get away*.

I jumped, too.

You heard me.

I jumped—even though I didn't have the benefit of a Kevlar line. Or a parachute.

Man, I was free-falling from fifty floors high, making up the plan as I flew.

Jane saw me, suitably stunned—and I hoped a little impressed.

I also hoped she wouldn't mind a little company.

I hurtled through the dark night, flying straight into her and grabbing hold of her wrists. We were now both hanging from the same rig.

My added weight slowed her down, till the line sagged and went slack.

There we dangled together in the middle of her escape line, arms and legs entwined in a survival grip, fifty floors above the goddamn street, where the city's glittering nightlife went on oblivious to our little drama. We were in limbo at deadly dizzying heights.

I *think* it was the height that was making me a little dizzy. Though I have to say Jane was the most delicious-feeling lifesaver I'd ever clung to before.

Naturally my ego was bruised a little when it became apparent that our sudden airborne embrace didn't affect her as much as it did me.

"You had a clear shot up there," she said. "You didn't take it. That was sweet. And suicidal."

Still planning to kill me, was she? Okay, so I was enjoying this little game of Twister more than she was. I slipped my hand into my pocket to grab my gun, but her hand clamped down on mine like a vise.

Damn, where'd she work out? She had a grip like a goddamn gorilla.

"You think you'd have known I was there if I didn't *want* you to?" I scoffed. "You're predictable, Jane. I can see you coming from a mile away."

She twisted her wrist, managing to slip her hand in my pocket—a move I rather enjoyed. Too bad it was my gun she was after.

"You never used to know when I was coming," she said, "so why start now?"

Bitch! I grabbed her arm and spun her on the rig,

so I ended up plastered to her from behind, my lips to her ears. "Maybe it's because you've begun to show an interest in me again."

She struggled against me, but the more we wrestled, the more we ground together, in a hot, sweaty, deadly embrace.

"You know," I growled in her ear, "we haven't been this close in years."

Hoo-hoo, that made her so mad, she managed to wriggle free and spin back around so we were face-to-face.

Which was fine with me. Personally, I think the missionary position is very underrated.

"Don't get too comfortable," she grated, twisting against me. A little breathlessly, I noticed. Was that from exertion or something else?

Frankly, I could have hung around like that for a while, but I was afraid we'd both pay the penalty for loitering if we didn't resolve the situation soon.

I crushed my body to hers, locking her arm against her sides so she couldn't aim up at me with the gun.

"Don't worry, I won't," I shot back. "Because you're leaving town."

She locked gazes with me, nose to nose, chest to chest, and . . . everything else to everything else. Then her eyes flashed. Definitely a hot look for her. "You really expect me to roll over and play dead?" she exclaimed.

"Why not?" I shot back. "I did for five years of marriage."

"*Six!*" she hissed.

I shrugged, giving her just enough leverage to pull an amazing move: arching her back, she freed her arm and leveled the gun at me.

"I'm not leaving," she stated flatly.

In answer, I pulled a pretty fucking amazing move of my own: Swinging and kicking upward, I managed to boot the gun out of her hand. Luck and skill, if I say so myself, enabled me to snatch it from the air on its way down.

"Neither am I," I said. I had the gun and the position. The best seat in the house, in fact. In more ways than one.

Poor kid. In a last effort of resistance, she whipped out a blade. Not a very impressive one at that.

I shook my head in disdain. "You of all people should know, Jane: You don't bring a knife to a gun-fight."

"Fight's over, John," she hissed as she slashed the knife through the air—not at my throat, as I feared!

Instead she sliced at the shared Kevlar rope above our heads that was keeping us up and alive—as opposed to down there and splattered like jack-o'-lanterns on the pavement.

Fuck! Was she trying to get us killed?

In the millisecond before the severed end of the cable swung back toward Jane's office building, I dropped my gun and grabbed onto it. I knew it was my only salvation.

Holy shit! Like Indiana Jones I raised my legs midswing as I sped toward a large office window.

Smash!!! Glass shattered all around me as I crashed through it, tumbled across the floor, and rolled up onto my feet in one smooth move. *Perfect ten, man,* I thought in that exhilaration that informs every atom of your body. *I'm not dead!*

Dusting off the debris, I turned back to the gaping

window and stared across the great divide. No sign of Jane.

I took a deep breath and made myself peek at the view below.

No crowds gathering; no unusual splatter on the ground either.

Amazing. She and I had both pulled our asses out of this one.

My wife was still out there, somewhere, plotting her next move.

My eyes narrowed. So be it.

I'd never faced a more challenging foe. The thrill of the hunt was still coursing through my veins. I was ready for the next phase of competition. *Bring it on, babe.*

I straightened out my clothes and turned to go, catching sight, for the first time, of an old cleaning lady quivering against the wall as she clutched her mop.

I actually blushed. "Sorry about the mess," I mumbled. And I meant it.

But I didn't have time to hang around and help her clean up.

I had a wife to kill.

JANE

It was a bold move to slash the line—a calculated risk. But what choice did I have? I was dangling by a gossamer thread over death's snapping jaws while carrying a lot of extra baggage—my soon-to-be ex-husband. Who, I might add, would not quit squirming all over me. I had to do something drastic if I was going to make it out of the situation alive.

So I embraced the gamble. I was airborne. All I had to do now was make damn sure I survived.

An instant memory flashed through my mind, a virtual movie of an elegant trapeze artist I once saw when I was little. That image inspired me now. If I was to survive, I could not think of myself as rushing headlong toward a steel-and-concrete building—a surface upon which I might smash like a summer bug on a speeding windshield. I had to believe that I was an aerialist *en leotard,* soaring above an adoring crowd (and a well-knotted safety net) toward the platform on the other side. I had to almost hear the music, almost smell the popcorn, and the elephants . . .

Milliseconds later I dropped onto a balcony, so gracefully the pigeons barely fluttered as I landed.

Safe! I instantly turned back to see what had happened to . . . to my adversary.

I gasped when I saw him.

I mean really. For six years I had been a golf widow. Married to a man who thought bending his drinking arm while driving around on a golf cart was exercise that deserved to be rewarded by another round of cocktails served poolside at the club.

This man flying through the air could not be my husband. This man who swung through the air by the end of a Kevlar cord like Tarzan on a vine.

Him Tarzan, me Jane . . .

Amazing. I knew from experience it wasn't easy to face a window knowing you were going to have to go through it still closed. *Not that face!* I thought. But he knew what he was doing. I watched him maneuver in the air to take it feetfirst.

I winced when he crashed through, worried when he went

down, and was amazed when he was on his feet again in one smooth move.

This could not be the same guy I'd been living with all these—

Good God! What was I doing? I didn't want to admire this man, or salivate over his skills and physique. He was a liar, a con man, a complete and utter fraud. I couldn't stand him!

With an angry shake of my head, I wound up my Kevlar line and looped it over my shoulder, then quickly ducked to pick the lock on the balcony door. I needed to get the hell out of there ASAP and reconnect with my team.

Damn him. I hoped he hadn't read my emotions as we dangled in midair. Or smelled my fear.

Not my fear of falling or dying.

My fear of him, and the disturbing effect he was having on me.

I mean, Christ. Those hot groping moments out there beneath the stars ...

It was the best sex we'd had in years.

And it sure lasted a lot longer.

I didn't know who the hell this man was, but I knew one thing: He was armed and dangerous, and I didn't have any kind of weapon that could protect me against that.

JOHN

I took refuge again at Eddie's house, where I paced like a caged tiger. Arteries pumping with adrenaline, muscles bunched, ready to spring—classic fight-or-flight syndrome.

But to flee or fight what? My own life for the past five years?

I felt shackled. Blinded by the intensity of

conflicting emotions, I was unable to see clearly, unable to explain.

I only knew I wanted to beat the crap out of somebody.

On top of everything else, Eddie was being a real jerk of a Monday-morning quarterback.

"You had the shot . . . ?"

He sat on his living-room couch in a ratty bathrobe, chain-smoking, while I sifted through a pile of equipment I'd hauled in from the burned rubble of Jane's office.

"I'm just saying, you had a clear shot, and you didn't take it?"

I didn't want to talk about it. So I just kept working, looking through the debris for . . . what? I don't know . . . something. Something that would make it all make sense.

Or maybe I was just procrastinating, putting off the inevitable.

"Jesus!" Eddie exclaimed. "This shit's from the goddamn Pleistocene era. Leave it overnight, we'll have diamonds."

"Just keep looking, Eddie," I said.

"For what? Fossils? Johnny. You don't have time to be mining here. They gave you forty-eight hours, so you got what, twenty-two, twenty-three left?"

I knew I was doing a James Dean. But I couldn't help it. I checked my watch. "Eighteen and change."

"Eighteen hours till they close the books on *both* of you. Johnny, no more games. You need to hit this bitch head-on—now!"

I glared at him. "Eddie. Don't tell me how to handle my wife."

Eddie shook his head in disgust. He was a real black-and-white kind of guy. "She's *not* your wife, John."

I slowed down as the words penetrated my brain.

"You gotta wrap your head around that," Eddie said, not unkindly. "This broad's *not* your wife. She's the *enemy*. Trust me, she's out there right now, scheming with her friends, sweating how to take you down . . . take your house, the car, the cat . . . the goddamn *Cuisinart—*"

"Eddie!" I said. He was losing it—heading off into the war zone of his own past relationships.

Suddenly I stopped and dusted off a tiny scrap of paper. Eddie moved in closer to see what it was. The tiny scrap had four letters: *TZKY.*

"How much to buy a vowel?" Eddie asked.

Maybe it was some kind of clue.

But Eddie just scoffed and continued to nag me about knocking off my wife. "You just gotta do it, man."

Yeah, but how? This wasn't some average broad I was dealing with. Not even your day-to-day professional killer. She was good, I thought with reluctant admiration. Damn good. Not that she could ever outwit *me.* But she *would* be a challenge.

Eddie hit me up hard with some no-holds-barred advice. "Get into her life now . . . into her head . . . find an in . . . *Go home,* brother."

Go home? Yeah, right. Where the hell was that?

I slowed my pacing. Go home. Hmm.

Ridiculous? Maybe not.

Would she even be there?

Maybe she was gone already. Or maybe she was there, thinking no way I'd ever show my face on that block again. Which would make her more vulnerable.

"And Johnny, bring a shield," Eddie warned. "A cover. Somebody to take that first bullet if she's locked and loaded in the fuckin' chimney."

I threw up my hands. "Where the hell am I going to find that kind of mark?"

Then I stopped, eyes narrowing. A face came to mind. The perfect shield, living very conveniently right under my nose.

I wasted no time showing up on my next-door neighbor's doorstep. We were buddies, after all, right? I rang the damn bell.

How many times over the past five years had I stood on this front porch with a bottle of wine or a six-pack of beer under my arm? Or holding a covered-dish entrée while Jane gave her makeup a final check?

The perfect suburban couple showing up for another benign suburban soiree.

Like that last one. Showing up at the last minute, breathless, with that look in her eyes.

I'd been so concerned about covering up what *I'd* been doing that I didn't even see what was going on with her. I thought she was a little nervous about going to the party.

Instead, she'd been fucking lying to me.

Where the hell had she been that night? What the hell had she been doing?

And who the hell had she been with?

The Colemans' garden gnome grinned at me, so I gave him a swift kick in the balls.

Shit. Whatever guilt I may have felt for what I was about to do was now smothered by a blinding-hot rage I couldn't extinguish. And couldn't quite define.

I jabbed the bell again.

Martin Coleman was unlucky enough to be home. *Bad karma, man,* I thought as he opened the door wearing one of those stupid white chef hats and a barbecue apron that read HOT TO TROT.

The guy was a fuckin' suburban moron.

"Aloha," I said cheerfully, slipping easily into my suburban-buddy slang.

It didn't take long to convince him to come next door with me. I think I muttered something about needing advice, come over for a drink . . . He was delighted. Eager, in fact.

I realized, with a tiny bit of conscience, that in spite of all the times I'd been to his home, I'd never once invited him to mine.

He practically jogged to my front porch. I carefully scanned the shrubbery for signs of weaponry aimed in our direction. But the azaleas looked clean.

I unlocked the front door and pushed it open with the toe of my shoe.

Silence greeted us.

The door swung open slowly, and I peered inside.

No sign of her.

Always the perfect host, I motioned for my shield—I mean, my guest—to enter first.

Martin Coleman stepped into my home as if he were entering Mar-a-Lago or something.

I braced, half expecting the front hall to explode.

Or at least his head.

But nothing happened.

"I can't believe I've never been in here before!" Martin exclaimed, looking around with unabashed curiosity.

I glanced around uneasily. Clever, I thought. Jane

was going to be subtle. Lure me in, hypnotize me into letting down my guard.

I followed Martin cautiously, keeping my head low, one hand on my holster.

"I love your floors!" Martin exclaimed. "Teak?"

I looked at the goddamn floors. "Fuck if I know. C'mon, I'll give you the full tour."

We were both wide-eyed as we moved through the menacing shadows of what used to be my home—Martin in nosy wonder, me in apprehension.

"Hey, you got the Masters Cup from the country club this year." Martin gushed, picking up the trophy from a shelf.

But I was too anxious to bask in his admiration.

Slowly we made our way into the living room.

Suddenly Martin let out a girlish yelp!

I stooped, gripping my gun behind my back, and scanned the room, but I saw nothing. *What?*

Martin pointed through the open powder-room door. "Dulcite faucets!"

Jesus Christ! I let out my breath and waved him ahead. "Knock yourself out, man."

As Martin darted into the john to admire the fixtures, I stole quietly up the stairs.

Gun hand ready, I pivoted into our bedroom. *The* bedroom, I corrected myself. *You don't live here anymore,* I reminded myself. *If you ever did . . .*

After a quick look behind the door and around the room, I rifled through Jane's drawers, looking for weapons or . . . I wasn't sure what else, really. Some kind of explanation, I guess. But the drawers were kind of empty—maybe she'd already cleaned out what little she wanted to keep from five years of marriage.

In fact, the whole place looked professionally ransacked. And I knew by who.

I moved to the closet next, leading with the nose of my gun, just in case. She'd left lots of clothes behind—costumes no longer needed from her suburban-wife persona. I snagged one of her silky night things on the tip of my gun.

Oh, yeah. I remembered this one.

Before I could stop myself, I'd drawn it to my face and closed my eyes.

It smelled like midnight, and rumpled bedclothes, and my wife . . .

Goddammit. "She's not your wife," I reminded myself. "She's not your wife."

I turned my head and spotted somebody lying in the corner—the stuffed bear she'd won at the street fair in Little Italy. *Beginner's luck,* she'd said.

Yeah, right.

Bear had had his guts ripped open.

Poor bastard. I knew how he felt.

Then I spotted something in the trash. A videotape.

I stored my gun in my waistband and reached for the tape, reading the label.

It was the videotape of our honeymoon.

My gut twisted. *"She's not your wife . . ."*

"So what's your secret?"

Startled, I nearly put a bullet in the intruder before I realized it was Martin. He stood in the doorway, staring at me.

Had he seen my gun? Had he discovered something in this house that revealed the secrets Jane and I had kept from each other for all these years?

"Come on, you can tell me," he said slyly. "We're neighbors."

I shrugged, feigning innocence.

Persistent, Martin winked and stepped forward into the room. "How do you keep things, you know . . . *spicy*?" He nodded toward my hands.

Jeez. I was still holding the video in one hand, the nightie in the other.

I stared at them and felt like ripping the silk, smashing the plastic against the wall.

But I couldn't lose my cool in front of a curious witness. Besides, I'd played tougher charades than this.

"Well, Martin," I said smoothly, "it's not easy. You've got to pay attention to each other. Study the details—"

I broke off when I spotted a notepad lying next to the phone on the bedside table. I could see the words from the previous note embedded in the top sheet.

Well, well, well.

"—and *never* underestimate the value of surprise."

I grabbed the pad, turned my back on Martin, and slipped a small breath-spray-size atomizer out of my coat pocket. A quick spritz of ultraviolet mist onto the sheet revealed the message: *LUBETZKY REAL ESTATE.* And an address.

I smiled. There were my mystery letters: *TZKY.*

Great. Obviously Triple-Click needed a new office after their unexpected fire yesterday. How convenient that Jane had left me a change of address.

I made up a quick excuse to my guest, told him I just remembered something I had to do, but promised that Jane and I would have both him and his wife, Suzy, over soon for cocktails or dinner. An easy enough lie.

I walked him back to his driveway, then made a

beeline for my toolshed. Once inside its cool darkness, I locked the door, grabbed a flashlight, then opened the trapdoor and dropped inside to find . . .

Nothing?! What the—?

I couldn't fucking believe it! My money, my weapons—*everything* was gone. Not even a pocketknife remained.

My secret arsenal had been totally cleaned out—by Jane and her happy little maid service, no doubt.

"Bitch!"

It was just the cold shower I needed to hose down my stupid surge of romantic sentimentality.

With new resolve, I climbed up the ladder and slammed the door on the emptiness.

I was a professional again.

And this was war.

JOHN

I rocked back on my heels to look at the brand-new skyscraper that rose eighty-some floors into the dazzling blue sky. Somebody had some money.

I checked the address on the slip of paper from Jane's notepad. Yep. This was the place. Floor 82.

I never knew the temp business was so damn profitable.

The building was still under construction, but I guess Triple-Click just couldn't wait to move in and get to work. Plotting my assassination, no doubt.

Dressed in black work clothes and carrying a beat-up toolbox, I was just another blue-collar calendar hunk on his way to work, and it was easy to slip in through the scaffolding.

Inside the elevator, I punched my floor and watched the numbers rise: 70, 71, 72 . . . 73 . . . 74 failed to light up . . . 75, 76 . . . and then the elevator suddenly stopped between floors.

I waited a moment, to see whether this was planned espionage or routine elevator crankiness. At last a male voice crackled over the speaker box: "This is security. There seems to be a problem with your elevator, sir. Would you like us to send up an engineer to take a look?"

"No, thanks," I replied. "I'm happy waiting here till it works itself out."

There was a pause. Then: "Is that sarcasm, sir?"

When I didn't answer, the guard spoke again, far too impatiently for a mere low-wage security guard: "*Is it?*"

In fact, his inflections reminded me very much of the impatient tone of my wife in an argument.

I smiled calmly into the security cam mounted on the wall. You never knew who might be watching you on these things.

Just for fun, I blew her a kiss.

JANE

So. He'd deciphered the address from the notepad I'd left lying on my bedside table at home. Now he was here. And I had no delusions about why he'd come or what he planned to do.

I stared at the surveillance footage of John stuck on the elevator between floors.

Damn. My husband always did look wicked good in black.

He's not your husband, I reminded myself.

I had spoken to him as a security guard, my voice altered by a modulator to sound like a man's. When he didn't answer my question, I repeated it: *"Is it?"*

He lifted his chin toward the monitor and looked me straight in the eye. And I was sure—modulator or no modulator—that he knew exactly who he was talking to.

Especially when he blew me a kiss.

Damn him.

I dropped the fake voice. "This is *your* first and last warning, John."

John smiled into the camera, and I thought I heard one of my younger crewmembers sigh. That crooked grin of his had always been his most effective weapon.

"You know I'm not going anywhere," John replied smoothly.

Well, he had guts, I'd say that much for him. It had eluded me as he drank and golfed and sleepwalked his way through our suburban confection of a life together. It doesn't take much courage to use a Weedwacker or take out the recycling.

"So you say," I countered. "But right now you're sealed in a steel box dangling over seventy-six floors of clear air."

We watched John yank on the doors. They didn't budge. Saw him check out the emergency hatch on the ceiling. Too high.

"What have you got up there?" John asked.

"Wouldn't you like to—"

"Shaped charge on the counterweight cable?" he ventured. "And two more on the primary and secondary brakes?"

"He found them," Julie said, surprised.

I smiled, impressed. "Not all of them," I told her, then I turned back to the mike. "John, did you also catch the base charge for the principal cable?"

His megawatt smile dropped to half-mast. He hadn't. "That'll teach me to take the express."

"You think I'm dumb enough to leave a sensitive number by

the side of the bed?" I scoffed. "And I thought you were *more* than just a pretty face."

That certainly wiped the grin off him. I tried not to gloat.

His face hardened, eyes boring into mine, and he shook his head. "You're not gonna blow it."

"Oh, no?"

"No."

We were playing a deadly game of poker; easy for me, but he was dangling in an elevator shaft.

"You think I won't?"

"I think you won't."

His answer was so quick, so sure, so insulting.

Suddenly my head roared with the pain and anger of his deceit. I turned to Jessie, my heart as hard as steel. And nodded.

Jessie instantly hit the keys. Green lights on the screen went red. Translation: *Armed.*

I began the countdown. "Five, four . . ."

"Why count down, Jane?" John challenged me. "If you're gonna blow it, blow it." He shrugged. "Three, two, one: Go."

Smart-ass! He was poking at me, and I hated to be poked. "Any last words?" I growled.

A wicked grin blossomed on his face. "I *hate* the new curtains."

Bastard!

"Good-bye, John."

If he'd been hoping for a soft heart or a governor's reprieve, he'd just blown it. I reached for the button that would blow that goddamn arrogant face to kingdom come—

That face, those eyes. That body. Those lips . . .

But then something happened. Something that hadn't happened since my first time, starting out.

I choked. My hand literally froze over the button.

God help me, but I couldn't do it.

I dropped my hand to my lap, horrified at myself.

I knew it! John's smug smile said.

It was unbearable.

But before I could think what came next, I heard a horrible sound:

Bang! Bang! Wham!

John looked stunned as he and I realized at the same time—the charges had exploded.

The two-ton elevator car was dropping like a ton of bricks.

I watched in horror as the force of the fall slammed him to the roof of the elevator car.

But my hand never touched that button! What the hell happened!? My head whipped toward the flashing word on Jessie's laptop: *RELEASE*.

My eyes blazed at her like twin nuclear explosions.

"What?" Jessie said. "You said good-bye."

I jumped to my feet and stared impotently at the screen. Rocked by the knowledge of what I knew was happening. Dizzy with horror . . . *Quick! Maybe I could . . .*

ZZZZZtttt! The monitor hissed at me, calling me *fool . . .*

John's face disappeared, replaced by a blank, static void.

JOHN

The car was dropping fast, speeding like a freight train toward the bottom of the shaft, the force throwing me to the roof of the car.

Yet I managed to smile good-bye to Jane as I passed through the hatch and landed on the top of the falling elevator.

The vibration knocked my toolbox over, spilling its contents everywhere, causing my tools to dance wildly around. I stuck my head back in the car—the Muzak version of "The Girl from Ipanema" was playing. I couldn't believe it. They were killing a perfectly good song.

I jumped down to get a pipe wrench that was skittering around and launched myself back to the roof, where I quickly wedged the wrench against what looked like a secondary brake mechanism. It wouldn't budge at first, then it gave way. Something happened. The car started to slow down. More and more.

Until finally it stopped. On the fourth floor. The number was stenciled on the inside of the door. I wondered how I was going to open it.

Bang!

Whatever was holding us gave out then.

And the elevator shot down the shaft, two tons of metal, slamming the ground with a deafening impact.

JANE

I did it. *Oh, my God.* I really did it.

I looked across the street at that beautiful new skyscraper as destruction erupted from its lobby doors.

Construction accident. That's what they'd call it. No one would ever know what really happened.

I was not even in the building at the time. My team and I were parked a safe distance away in our black van—a mobile command center from which I'd orchestrated the whole thing. In fact, John had walked right past us on his way into the building and never realized that we weren't talking to him from the eighty-second floor.

One could argue that, technically, I *didn't* do it—that Jessie had set off the explosions.

But I'd planned the whole thing. I'd set the charges myself. And I was the one who left an imprint of the address on a notepad by my bed. That clue was so fourth-grade Nancy Drew, but John fell for it like one of those dopey Hardy Boys.

The whole thing was a setup. And he'd walked straight into our trap.

So what if at the last moment it wasn't my finger that actually pressed the key that triggered his annihilation?

I'd planned to strike the key. I'd orchestrated the whole thing. The blood—John's blood—was on my hands.

I felt . . . what? Horror? Remorse? . . . Grief?

I don't know. Dazed, mostly, like someone who wakes up from sleepwalking in the middle of a strange place.

How did I get here?

I finally heard sirens screaming as cops and emergency crews swarmed toward the wreckage.

But I knew they'd need no ambulance.

I'm good at what I do. And I was positive there'd be no clues left behind.

And no body . . .

He was gone. John . . . was gone.

Police lights danced across our faces like lights in a surreal disco. Beside me, Jasmine studied my expression.

But I turned away before she could see what I was feeling.

I was a professional. Like a heart surgeon, I couldn't afford to feel anything if I wanted to do my job successfully.

My eyes shot back to the scene across the street. Yes, I did it.

And it was exactly what he'd have done to me if I hadn't done it first.

JOHN

She did it," I gasped. "She really did it."

It took a few moments to convince myself that I wasn't in heaven—or hell. That I was still alive, hanging by my fingertips to a ledge four floors above the wreckage.

Wreckage that should have included bits and pieces of my skull and ass.

Jesus Christ. She did it.

Somehow, I hadn't believed that she would. That she could, in the end.

But she did. Guess she figured if she didn't do me, I'd sure as hell do her.

Would I have?

If I'd had one last shot, would I have pulled the trigger and blown her brains out before she sent me plunging to hell?

Well, John?

Jesus. She did it. She fucking did it.

Now. I had to tap into some of that adrenaline I was wasting on wanting to kill her and use it to get out of here—to get even.

JANE

another taxi ride through the city streets. Lights glittering like diamonds in the crisp night air.

I'd quickly showered, changed: a well-trained assassination machine transitioning out of a mission. I'd packed away my guns and computers for new tools: lipstick, eyeliner, a new dress, heels.

The cab pulled up to a curb and a doorman helped me out,

and as I approached the entry to one of New York's most elegant restaurants, I gazed at my reflection in the plate-glass window: The dress flattered me—black, feminine, sexy. I had turned back into Jane Smith—woman, wife.

No, my heart reminded me. *Not wife.*

Widow.

God, I needed a drink. I hurried inside, barely noticing the appreciative glances that followed me as the maître d' led me to my table. A table for two.

"Champagne, please," I murmured as he seated me.

"Very good, Mrs. Smith."

They knew me here. John and I had dined here often; it was— *had been*—one of our favorite places.

I blinked away the troublesome moisture gathering in my eyes and surveyed the place—part instinct and training, part curiosity. The room seemed to overflow with happy people. Friends, families, couples in love . . . or, at least, *with* someone.

I was not unfamiliar with being by myself. I'd been on my own most of my life, even as a child.

But tonight . . . I had never felt more *alone.*

I closed my eyes and took a long drink of my champagne— the sparkling wine of celebration—willing the effervescence to fill my spirit. Didn't I have much to celebrate, after all?

I had survived the disintegration of a situation that was no longer productive.

Hah. That was a good line. I'd have to write it down.

But really. Marriages fell apart all the time these days—over much smaller conflicts. Hell, mine had been a goddamn war— with real guns and explosives. There was no way we could have simply gone our separate ways. Ours was definitely a "take no prisoners—leave no witnesses" kind of relationship.

Till death do us part.

Funny how you never really think about those words in the passion of saying *I do.*

So our mad love-and-war games had been fought to the finish. I had won. And I was lucky to be alive.

But as I set my glass down on the luxurious white tablecloth, the untouched place setting and the empty chair seemed to mock me.

And I could not will my heart to celebrate.

Laughter invaded my thoughts, and I sought the source like a dying woman seeking water. I shouldn't have looked: The sounds radiated from a young couple in the corner, young lovers immersed in each other's adoration, oblivious to everything around them, including the look of pure envy I'm sure I wore on my face.

I reminded myself not to long for things I would never have and reached again for my empty glass.

Reading my mind, a waiter appeared behind me to pour more champagne.

"Thank you," I murmured, blinking to clear my vision.

"Madam."

God, he sounded so much like John.

I looked up into the man's face—and nearly cried out!

It *was* John! Alive, all in one piece . . . But how . . . ?

Champagnelike bubbles danced at the edges of my vision, tempting me with temporary escape.

But I held on and returned his gaze.

My God, he was not only alive, he looked positively devastating in a dark suit and tie. Very pulled together for a man who had just cheated death.

Most wives who'd just killed their husbands would have shown some surprise. But years of training and experience kicked in, carrying me forward on a wave until I could gain control. My hand trembled slightly as I raised my glass to my lips, but I took a long sip as if I'd been waiting for him all along.

I waited for him to speak first.

"I thought of a number of lines for this moment," he said at last. "'Thought I'd drop in . . .' or 'Hey, doll, thanks for giving me the shaft . . .'"

I swallowed my champagne and casually asked, "Which did you settle on?"

His eyes bored into mine. "I want a divorce."

Ooph. Body blow.

My face? Close-up, Oscar-winning performance in the devastating role of a lifetime: Turning my best side to the camera, I cocked my head thoughtfully, as if considering his choice. "I like it," I replied. "You proposed to me here, so there's an agreeable symmetry to it."

John pulled out the empty chair. "May I sit?"

"Please."

As he seated himself and shook out his napkin to place in his lap, a real waiter appeared. "Champagne, sir?"

John's eyes never left mine. "Champagne is for celebrating."

He paused long enough for me to remember: It was the same thing he'd said the night he proposed.

But now he added pointedly: "I'll have a martini."

John's performance was crisp, controlled, a bit on the Clark Gable side. *This should be a movie,* I thought.

Holding his gaze, I delivered my next line: "Better make it two."

The waiter whisked away my champagne glass and disappeared.

As John studied my face over the candlelight, I worked hard to appear as beautiful and as uncaring as possible.

"You kept my place setting," he said at last. "You weren't expecting me, were you?"

I shrugged. "Call me sentimental."

"Surprised?"

"That you had time to shave?"

"That I haven't fired yet."

I laughed. For two people who were intent on murdering each other, we sure were a hell of a lot alike.

I should have guessed he'd be packing more than the family jewels beneath his linen napkin.

Hadn't I, the seasoned professional, done the same? On reflex, I'd sneaked a finger gun from a garterlike holster on my thigh and cloaked it beneath the napkin on my lap. At this very moment it was aimed directly at his . . . brains.

"Not really," I replied.

Thus we acknowledged that we both knew we were both packing. We smiled like enemies whose skill makes them strange comrades.

"My favorite part of dining out," John quipped. "Witnesses." He smiled a truce. "Hands on the table?"

Dare I trust him? I thought.

Of course not.

But we were in the middle of a posh restaurant. A place where we were well known. It would be such an awkward place for a murder. Not to mention that whoever survived would never be able to get a reservation here again.

Slowly I withdrew my hands from my lap and placed them on the table. John's actions mirrored my own.

If you're not here to blow me away, John, then why are you here?

I decided to get the business part of the evening out of the way over cocktails, before we ordered. The chef here rocked, and I was suddenly absolutely ravenous. "So," I began. "You're here to discuss terms."

We paused as the waiter delivered our martinis. John knocked his back without our usual toast. Then he leaned forward as if he were telling me how beautiful I looked.

"We have an unusual problem, as I see it. You obviously want me dead, and I must admit, your longevity is becoming less and less a priority for me." He rubbed his chin thoughtfully. "We could each open fire and hope for the best."

"That would be a shame," I pointed out. "I'm sure they'd ask me to leave once you were dead."

John's eyes smoldered, the air crackled between us.

"So the problem becomes *these*"–John held up his hands, a smile teasing his lips–"and what to do with them."

I squirmed in my seat. John did have wonderful hands. And at the moment, I could think of several things he could do with those hands, but none of them had anything to do with our problem.

It was definitely getting warm in here. And then a single note from an alto sax insinuated itself between us, tying us up in its smoky tones.

A lazy smile blossomed on John's handsome face, seducing one from me.

"Dance?" he murmured.

I didn't hide my surprise. We hadn't danced once since that first night in Bogotá. "I thought you didn't like to–"

"Part of my cover."

"Was sloth part of it, too?"

But he just stood, holding out his hand in invitation.

As I placed my hand in his and rose from my chair, he whispered in my ear, "Leave 'em at the table?"

I nodded, and we both adjusted our linen-cloaked guns.

Suddenly John pulled me into a passionate embrace. Startled, I didn't resist as his hands roamed my body–shoulders, waist, hips . . .

It was the hottest frisk I'd ever endured.

"Just checking," he said huskily.

"Satisfied?"

"Not for years."

Bastard!

Livid, I spun him around and shoved him up against the wall

behind a potted fern. (Hours in the agency gym had given me a lot more than curves.) Pressed against him, the jazz a smoky sound track to our complicated skirmish, I forced him to endure the same maddening torture he'd performed upon me. My hands rambled across his chest, down his broad muscular back, along his marvelous hips . . . into his pockets . . .

I flushed. Was that a gun in his pocket, or was he just glad he hadn't killed me yet?

Distracted, I foolishly dropped my guard, which allowed John to escape my hold and strong-arm me onto the dance floor. I tried to twist free, but he was in control this time, and imprisoned me against the hard planes of his body.

"You think this story has a happy ending?" he whispered roughly as we began to move to the music.

I fought the pleasure of his breath upon my neck. "Happy endings are just stories that haven't finished yet."

In response, he spun me across the floor in a heated embrace.

And we danced.

A mating dance or a duel . . . who knew?

Whatever it was, he knew all the steps in this wordless tango of passion, anger, regret . . . pain.

The man was torturing me here, in full view of the world.

So I did what I'd long ago learned to do when I was hurting. I fought back.

"Why is it, you think, that we failed?" I goaded him. "Was it because we were living separate lives? Or was it all the lying that did us in?"

"I have a theory," John said. "Newly realized."

"I'm breathless to hear it."

His hands tightened on my hand, my waist. "*You* killed us."

A poison dart to my heart. "Provocative," I replied.

But he'd only begun. "Your aloofness, your arctic efficiency, especially in bed—" He plunged me backward into a dramatic dip, and I hung there helplessly, in his arms, my eyes glittering with barely contained rage. "You approached our marriage like a job," he continued, "something to be reconned, planned, and executed—not lived."

Humiliated, furious, I hauled myself out of the submissive position and spun away, but with a yank, he reeled me back into his arms like a yo-yo on a string. And there he held me prisoner—my back to his chest, my body snuggled into his hips, his chin tucked into my shoulder.

"And you," I shot back, "*avoided* it. Your drinking, your monastic devotion to pinball . . ."

He spun me across the floor again, this time chauffeuring me into shadows, where we paused, breathless and sweaty, in each other's arms.

He wanted me face-to-face, now, and raw.

"What do you care," he demanded, towering over me, "if it was just a cover?"

He held me so tight I could barely breathe, and the words fell from my lips: "Who said you were just a cover?"

I thought he might crush me in response. "Wasn't I?" he ground out.

I swallowed. "Well . . . was *I*?"

"*You say first.*"

The saxophone wailed through my blood like cocaine, pounding my heart into my throat. John impaled me with his eyes, brainwashing me with his body in a hot grinding embrace.

Who is this man, and what has he done with my boring husband?

"Okay," John whispered. "On the count of three."

I nodded mutely.

"One, two . . . *three.*"

I could feel his heart beating, strong and fast, as we clung to each other, suspended there in the shadows. And for a moment, I almost thought . . . almost felt . . . almost hoped . . .

But the words . . .

There were no words . . .

Have you ever fought your way up from a nightmare and felt your jaw lock, found your lips sealed tight, no matter how desperately you tried to cry out?

That was my nightmare, there, in John's arms. I tried to cry out to him. But something held me back.

And every second of his silence ensured another moment of my own. Until our silence tore us apart.

The cold hard truth lay between us like a sword, severing all ties, and it spoke without words.

And I could see the answer in his eyes.

No happy endings.

I could no longer bear to be in his arms, and yet I could not pull away. John seemed unable to release me.

I don't know how long we stood there. But then the music ended, people were clapping and wandering back to their tables, and the spell was broken.

Our dance was over.

For always.

"Jane," John rasped out, his voice cold and hard, "we can end it here or we can end it outside. But it ends here."

"Then let me go!" I cried.

"I already have."

His words tore my heart.

Fool. What I had thought I'd felt in his touch, seen in his eyes, was just a mirage. Real to me; nothing but a professional game of strategy to him. And at that moment, I realized what was so awfully wrong with this picture.

John had let me go already. But I still hadn't let go of him.

And the terrifying truth was: I wasn't sure if I ever could.

I glanced away, feeling as if I were going to shatter like a champagne glass smashed upon the floor. I struggled to find the strength that had sustained me all these years.

At last I tore myself from John's arms and asked a nearby waiter: "Excuse me, where's the ladies' room?"

"Just over there, madam."

"Thank you."

And then I simply walked away, struggling not to stumble, not to break out into a full-fledged run.

I could feel John's eyes on me as I left him. Felt a heat that I knew must be hatred.

I had given up caring what most people thought of me long ago.

So why did this hurt so much?

JOHN

She walked away so easily, as if I were a stranger she'd just picked up for a dance.

How could she be so cold after all we'd just said, after all we'd just felt in each other's arms . . . What I thought we'd felt.

Obviously it was one-handed applause.

I watched her walk away, wanting to hate her, intoxicated by her body as it swayed in that slinky black dress, her hair as it moved softly about her shoulders. I watched her, remembering how she'd smelled in my arms, like a tropical flower on a hot night.

If only she would look back, just once . . .

But she never did.

My fists clenched at my sides. "Be cold, John. She's a liar. Be supercold."

The lines of a Robert Frost poem echoed in my mind: " 'Some say the world will end in fire, some say in ice.' "

To me, it felt like both.

JANE

J managed to make it through the ladies'-room door before my emotions escaped on a sob. I wasn't even sure what my feelings were. But one thing I knew for sure.

I was a goddamn fool for feeling them.

I caught my reflection in the mirror but didn't recognize the fragile, wounded woman who peered back.

I looked like a runaway from a romance novel.

Sorry, sister, I told her, grabbing a tissue to erase the tears. *I only read James Bond.*

I touched up my makeup and scolded myself for letting my guard down.

I was also kicking myself for leaving my gun back at the table. That was so not me.

Now what?

At the end of the room a matronly attendant leaned against the wall beside an array of complimentary toiletries: perfumes, mouthwashes, hair sprays, and lotions. Even free cigarettes. Along with the necessary matches, of course.

I quickly studied the offerings.

"Good evening," the attendant said with a smile that hoped for a nice tip.

"Evening," I replied. And then an idea came to me.

"Look what you have here," I said to the woman as I began to pick up bottles and read the ingredients. "Do you have any idea how many of those things are *flammable?*"

The attendant's smile slipped a little, unsure how to respond.

I grinned and rubbed my hands together.

I was one girl who knew how to play a killer game of beauty parlor.

JOHN

My eyes were glued to that ladies'-room door like a tick on a dog. No way that woman was giving me the slip.

I knew this place inside and out. Yeah, I'd even been in the ladies' room.

Don't ask.

So I knew there were no windows. And I knew Jane was too smart to try for the back door—no one would dare cut through this chef's kitchen, unless they wanted their head blown off.

No way out except right into my arms, babe.

I waited, glanced at my watch. She sure was taking a hell of a long time, even for a woman. I wondered if she was okay. Maybe she was more upset than that Stepford wife face of hers revealed. I was just about to go check on her when . . .

The ladies'-room attendant came flying past me like a bat out of hell, looking like she'd just seen the devil himself.

Or *her*self?

Uh-oh.

I reached for my gun—damn! Still on the table! Before I could turn to get it—

Blam! The floor shook. Chandeliers swayed. Smoke poured through the door of the john.

Jesus—then the whole damn room went nuts. Alarms shrieked. Sprinklers came on. People screamed, knocking over chairs as they scrambled for the exits.

I reached the table and grabbed my gun, then tried to make my way through the crowd, but the mob had become hysterical by then.

That's when I saw her, head down, slipping by the hostess station up front. I struggled to catch up to her, barely able to move, while she slipped through the crowd like a ghost.

But I managed to keep my eye on her the whole time. She didn't even glance back once to see if I was still there, if I was okay. But why would she? The fireworks were hers, a cover for her escape. A celebration of her independence.

Hell if I was going to let her get away.

I lifted a stout hyperventilating matron out of my way and fought toward the door.

At last I made it out onto the street—only to see Jane scratch off in the Benz.

Shit! I kicked at the air, frustrated as hell.

She did it again.

Now what? I stared after her, wondering what to do.

I felt a timid tap on my shoulder and whirled around.

"Excuse me," another escapee from the restaurant said apologetically, "but are you . . . ticking?"

I glared at the guy. The asshole must be drunk as hell. But I didn't have time for—

Tick-tick-tick . . .

Goddamnsonofabitch—I *was* fuckin' ticking!

It was somewhere in my jacket, but where? And when the hell had she planted it?

Christ, I'd been panting over her like a dog while she'd used her hot-mama act to cover a plant.

The ticking surrounded me. Screw it! I shimmied out of my jacket and tossed it—

Boom!

Bits of my suit coat scattered like confetti with the breeze.

The guy who'd tapped me on the shoulder squeaked from beneath a mailbox.

Now I was *really* pissed.

I loved that suit!

JANE

Escape. *But from what—to where?*

I'd done a cute Houdini act at the restaurant, but my heart was still tied up in ropes and chains.

Where could I run to from here?

I downshifted the Mercedes to take a turn. God, I loved this car, loved to drive it, especially at night. That's when I could most easily convince myself that life wasn't meaningless, that I was going *somewhere*, as long as I was moving forward, *fast*.

But tonight it wasn't helping. My lips still tasted like champagne, my hair smelled like smoke. I was a schizophrenic basket case. What the hell was I doing?

For the past six years my life had made sense. On the one hand I'd had my work, the danger, the thrill; on the other, an orderly, beautiful house, covered-dish parties at the neighbors', and a neatly clipped lawn. His-and-her towels, and toothbrushes. Dinners at seven.

I'd always tried to file, organize, and compartmentalize my life. I'd tried to be the best agent, the best wife, the best lover... but given the way I'd grown up, I wouldn't know a happy home if it bit me on the ass, so I'd designed everything after some perfect world I'd seen while peeking through other people's windows, into other people's lives.

Mine had only looked perfect on the outside. Somehow something was always missing, but I could never quite figure out what it was.

Now my two tidy parallel universes were all mixed up—the lines had been blurred. All files had been tossed in the air.

My life was out of control, and it scared me—a thought that would have made my coworkers at Triple-Click laugh. "Jane Smith isn't afraid of anything," they'd tell you. But they were wrong. This unraveling of my world frightened the hell out of me.

I clicked on the radio, searching for some mindless chatter to displace these destructive thoughts. A husky-voiced late-night talk-show host was trying to help a woman who complained that the magic had gone out of her marriage.

I started to change the channel, but the caller's words made me pause.

"I do everything," the woman complained. "I work outside the home, I hit the gym on my lunch hour so my figure's better than ever, I put a home-cooked meal on the table every night, my kids are straight-A students, and my house—you could eat off the floor, it's so clean."

"So what's your concern?" the host asked. "Does your husband drink?"

"Not more than average."

"Beat you?"

"No!"

"Cheat on you?"

"Never."

"Then what's the problem, Jane?"

Great—her name was Jane, too.

"Every night my husband sits down across from me at the dinner table and looks through me like I'm not even there."

"Um-hmmm," the host said. "You know what you need to do, Jane?"

"What?" I whispered, along with the other Jane.

". . . you should forget the damn pot roast, send the kids to Grandma's, and try cooking in bed, sweetheart. Stop focusing on the house! Who cares? Stop slaving over a hot stove. It's just food, honey. You can get it at any corner deli. Listen, Jane—perfect is about as sexy as the Bush administration. Sex is about wildness and mystery. It's about disorder—even danger. It's a terrifying ride at the amusement park that turns you upside down and takes your breath away—and if you let yourself lose control, you'll see stars, baby."

"Oh, but I—"

"Believe me, Jane—and all you other Janes listening out there tonight—if your perfect life is leaving you cold, then perhaps your life has become a caricature of your fantasy. You've got to shake it up a little, ladies. Lose the paint-by-numbers act and try painting like Jackson Pollock! Make a mess, for God's sake! Leave your husband's clothes on the floor—*after* you tear them off him! And another thing—"

Hands trembling, I hit the search button.

A deep male voice was now saying, ". . . I'll be taking you on a slow, sexy ride long into the night, with *Jazz for Lovers* . . . And remember, we're up as long as you're up . . ."

Give a girl a break! I reached to turn off the radio altogether when my cell phone rang.

Who—?

John.

Could he be calling?

I flipped open my cell and read my caller ID.

It *was* him.

My heart danced like a caffeine overdose. But don't ask me whether it was a good thing or a bad thing.

I hesitated, then answered the call. "Hello?"

"That's the *second* time you've tried to kill me."

Damn, he could run a successful phone-sex business with that voice. Thank God, I'd just slowed down for a stoplight. "Oh, please," I said sarcastically, playing it cool. "It was just a *little* bomb."

"I want you to know," he growled, "I'm going home and *burning* every single thing you ever bought."

I gunned my motor. He might as well have said *I'm coming home to make love to you till you scream bloody murder,* for the effect it had on me.

I smiled hungrily; I had skipped dinner, after all.

The light was still red, but who the hell cared? There was no one else in sight, and maybe the radio gal was right. A little danger, a terrifying ride—

"Race you there," I purred, and hit the gas.

JOHN

Hell, she could run a bang-up phone-sex business with that voice of hers.

My pulse was racing. From danger? Excitement? Or something else?

I didn't stop to analyze it; I just knew I had to get my hands on my would-be killer before this night was through. I'd figure out the rest of it once I'd jumped her.

A black sedan had just pulled up to the curb. The driver poked his head out of the window. "Limo, sir?"

I sized up the car. Just what the doctor ordered.

Moments later I was speeding through traffic onto the highway, one hand on the steering wheel, my cell phone in the other. Let's just say I'd given the limo driver the rest of the night off.

Hope he doesn't get a ticket for my driving, I thought. I had a date, and hell if I was going to be late.

Soon the road stretched out before me, taking me

back to what I used to call home. My lovely wife would be waiting for me, as usual.

But not as usual.

Umm.

If my wife was a different woman than I thought she was, was she still my wife?

I stared at the road ahead.

I glanced at my phone.

Eyes back on the road.

Back on the phone.

"Fuck it," I muttered, and speed-dialed.

Jane—who else would I be calling?—took her god-damned time answering.

"You're not *there* yet?" she said. Not even a hello.

"I need to know one thing," I said bluntly. "The first thing you thought the first time we met."

Dead silence. For once, no answer, no clever come-back.

I'd caught her off guard.

"You first," she said at last.

Oh, hell. Not this friggin' game again.

I was sick of games. Our whole goddamn marriage had been a game. For once, I just wanted to play it straight.

"I thought you looked like Christmas morning," I said. "I don't know how else to say it."

I thought the silence would stretch into eternity. Then: "Why are you telling me this now?"

"I . . ." *Christ. Why the hell was I?* "I guess, at the end, you start thinking about the beginning."

She didn't speak. I could hear the sounds of the traffic coming over her phone. She must be driving with the windows down, I thought; I could picture her hair in the wind.

"I just thought you should know the truth," I said.

Still no response.

Had she fallen asleep? Stopped for gas? Was she even listening? I wanted to shout at her. *Speak to me, Jane. Goddammit! Say something!*

"So tell me," I demanded. "Truth."

"I thought . . . I thought . . ." Her voice was soft and tender now.

"Yes?" I whispered.

"I thought you were the most beautiful—"

Her voice broke, and my chest felt like a fist unfolding.

But I must have misread her. Because the tenderness left her voice and she finished with: ". . . *mark* I had ever seen."

I nodded once in the dark car, digesting her words. Tasting them.

They tasted like crap. "It was all business," I said. Daring her to deny it. "From the go."

"All business," she said. "Cold. Hard. Math."

Just kick me in the balls, why don't you.

I decided to change lanes, into the speed zone. And the pathetic-looking guy I saw in my rearview mirror as I made my move? Funny, but he looked a lot like me.

I had to thank her, though. Thank her for keeping her head, and for giving me the chance to clear mine. "Thanks," I said briskly. "That's what I needed to hear."

I hung up, my armor back in place.

There was work to be done. No room for Hallmark cards on this job.

I stomped on the gas.

JANE

Christmas morning. He said I looked like *Christmas morning.*

We spend the last years of our marriage boring each other to death, acting like a couple of preprogrammed Animatronic mannequins from Disney World, and he waits till NOW to hit me with something like that?

I couldn't deal with it. Passion, anger, fear—sex—I could deal with just about anything.

But not a line like that.

He'd left the door open, and I had looked through it with longing . . . but I was too scared. He'd shown himself to be a liar of major proportions. He played deadly games with cold detached skill. I could no longer tell who he was, what was real, and what was just a devious strategy.

So in the end, something held me back.

JOHN

Here at last—home sweet fucking home.

I crested the last hill like a skateboarder taking flight over a mondo ramp.

But she was already there, just pulling into the driveway.

I couldn't let her get inside the house first, so I took a shortcut, tearing up the lawn as I T-boned across the front yard, and showered her Benz with dirt clods. I missed her expression as she jumped from her car, but I knew that move would drive her nuts. Screw it—she wasn't the one who mowed the lawn three times a week.

I cut the motor and scurried from the car, leaping over hedges to beat her to the front door.

I grinned in victory as I reached for the knob.

"Shit!" It was locked and bolted, and I didn't have my keys.

I whirled around to face her coming up the walk—but she was already slipping in the side door.

Christ! This house would be like a fortress to an experienced agent like Jane. I had to get inside.

I raced toward the backyard. I could probably bust down the door.

But as soon as I rounded the side of the house, the back door squeaked open.

There stood Jane, like a goddamn Amazon—hair whipping in the wind, eyes flashing in the moonlight, feet planted wide in a Rambo "don't fuck with me" posture.

A hunkin' submachine gun was cradled in her arms.

I froze right where I stood.

Well, most of me did. Damn, she looked hot.

I had no doubt she knew how to use the ammo. But would she?

Could she look me in the eye and blow me away, after the tortured dance we'd had earlier? After the things I'd said over the phone? She was a woman, after all. Even if she hated my guts, could she actually pull the trigger?

Jane moved, and I knew, the answer was—

FUCKING HELL YES!

I leaped away—

Blam!

Hell hath no fury like a woman . . .

I lay on the ground spitting dirt, preparing to die—knowing that, no matter how fast I crawled, rolled, or dug, she would blow me away. And I was hers on a plate.

But then, nothing happened.

I was relieved to find my head hadn't exploded. Surprised when she stepped back inside and slammed the door shut. I heard the lock click, heard her throw the bolt.

Stay out of my house, it said.

Sorry, Mrs. Smith, I muttered as I scrambled to my feet. *But my name's still on the deed.*

It wasn't the first time I'd had to break into my own house, but I was a little more sober this time. And I knew from experience, the basement provided the easiest access. I tore across the grass to the storm door, ripped it open, and was in. Then I bounded up the stairs, slipped through the door, and darted like a shadow toward my den.

Once inside my personal sanctuary, I popped open a panel hidden in the wall and pulled out a beautiful, ready-to-fire, shrink-wrapped silenced pistol.

No need to distract the neighbors from their reality TV.

Then I stepped into the hall.

It was too damn quiet. And eerie—the familiar spaces of my home suddenly felt like alien terrain. Did she know I was inside? Was she stalking me? Maybe she thought she'd scared me off with her angry display of firepower. Maybe she thought she was safe inside her bolted fortress and had gone to bed.

Well, babe, I've never let a woman's defenses keep me out of someplace I wanted to go.

I took a step toward the stairs.

Then saw a flash out of the corner of my eye. Was it Jane darting by?

BLAMBLAMBLAMBLAMBLAM . . .

I ducked as bullets ripped across the wall, shattering framed photos, busting a sconce.

Okay, she was still up. And still pissed as hell.

I ran for the nearest shelter—the kitchen—with Jane still hot on my heels. I turned and fired back, then leap-rolled over the kitchen island.

Jane fired again, but I yanked open the refrigerator door. Her bullets bounced off the Sub-Zero like it was a Greek warrior's shield.

Ouch. If she hadn't wanted to kill me before, she sure would now. She loved her fridge. It took her three months to get that model.

Then something inside it caught my eye. Oh, man. There was still some of that key lime pie of hers left. Instantly I salivated like Pavlov's dog, especially since Jane's fireworks display at the restaurant had made me miss dinner. I had to have some!

I was just wondering how I could reach the silverware drawer without getting my hand blown off when—

Blam! Blam!

Oh, yeah. Killer wife on rampage.

Damn—the pie would have to wait.

Maybe it was time to move into the dining room. As I moved toward the door, I fired off a round of shots. Elegant glasses exploded in a row, like bottles in a shooting gallery at a county fair. Cabinets blew open, spilling their gourmet guts. Her treasured teapot took a hit; and so did its companion, the teakettle. It would never whistle again.

Jane paused long enough to stare in disbelief at the destruction in her favorite room of the house: appliances, cabinets, decorative items—her precious kitchen was completely demolished.

Then she turned on me, and in her blistering gaze, I saw the fiery depths of hell.

Okay, can't stand the heat, I'm getting the hell out of the kitchen.

I stumbled toward the door, firing behind me, and then—*Click! Click! Click!*—oh, shit. I came up empty.

I took one look at Demon Woman and fled through the nearest exit.

Back out in the dark yard again.

But instead of coming after me, Jane just slammed the door once more and locked it.

"Dammit!" How'd she keep doing that? I felt like I was in some kind of bizarre Looney Tunes cartoon.

Shut out, in the dark, without a weapon.

This was not good. She was whipping my ass, and if word ever hit the streets about this, she was going to ruin my rep in the business.

I ran to my toolshed hoping to find another weapon. I knew she and her gang had cleared out my arsenal, but maybe I could find something makeshift among my tools.

Screwdriver—too iffy. Weedwacker—too gory. Insecticide—would take too long to kill.

I rummaged through the junk for something, anything—old paint cans, tattered life jackets, stack of old newspapers, a rusty bike. Jeez, I really needed to clean this place out.

Then my eyes settled on something with possibility: a big-ass pair of gardening shears.

I felt the weight of them in my hands—good and heavy. And versatile. I could pound, pry, stab, or cut. Not as high-tech as the gear I was used to, but under the circumstances, I figured they would serve me well.

I stepped back out under cover of darkness, waving

the shears around like a samurai waving his sword. But when I got to the basement door this time, I couldn't get in. Damn! Little Miss Efficient must have run down and padlocked it.

I could probably still get in, but it would take some time, and it'd make a hell of a lot of noise. So I opted to look for an alternative.

I snuck around the house, peeking through windows. I knew Jane was on the prowl, but at the moment, I didn't see any sign of her.

The den, I told myself. *She never goes in there.*

Or at least . . . I didn't *think* she did. Hell, maybe she went in there at night and danced naked on my desktop while her secret-agent lover prowled through my drawers. How the hell could I be sure of anything anymore?

I crept over to the den and risked a look. It was empty. No sign of desktop dancing. The window was locked, but I managed to slip the point of my garden shears in between the sill and the frame to crack it open.

They really didn't build houses like they used to.

Still no sign of Jane, so I climbed in. Shears first.

I got my bearings, then headed back to the kitchen. I figured she'd have fled by now, unable to bear the mess. Once there, I grabbed a shiny pan. Then paused. My eye caught a glimpse of something even better—a heavy-duty copper frying pan. Jane always did buy the best.

Now I headed back into the battle—armed with my trusty shears and my ever-loyal fryer.

Hey, like they say, it's not what you've got, it's what you do with what you have.

Slowly I moved into the living room, domestic weapons in hand, spinning slowly, covering every corner, checking behind every piece of furniture.

So far, so good.

Then I took one step into the foyer, and . . . *BANGBANGBANG!*

Like a sniper, Jane fired on me from the top of the stairs.

I ducked back into the living room, hung close against the wall, waiting.

Dead silence.

After a minute I quietly extended the shiny frying pan around the corner, to see if I could check out Jane's position in its mirrored surface.

Blam!

She shot the fucking pan right out of my hand and sent it flying across the room.

That's when it really hit me: why this whole operation was more dangerous than usual.

Most times when I had a target, I had a plan, I followed the plan, I went after the target. Cold, confident, efficient. Uninvolved. When the guy fought back, it was just survival. Nothing personal—for him or me.

But this thing with Jane—maybe it had started as a routine assignment from her Father, just like mine was a hit ordered by Atlanta.

But now—it was totally personal. And that's when things got dangerous.

I felt a pair of eyes on me, and spun around, shears raised in front of me.

Damn. I almost laughed.

There was her stuffed bear, leaning up against the fireplace, and despite his wounds, he was smiling at me like I was his long-lost buddy. So were all of

Jane's little figurines lined up on the shelves. She must have been gathering a few cherished mementos of our life together to take with her when she left.

Or to burn in the bonfire of the century.

Either way, it gave me an idea.

JANE

Sweating, I stopped to reload.

Then I plastered myself to the wall at the top of the stairs, listening for footsteps, the click of a gun hammer, a stomach growling, a burp—anything that might give away my adversary's position.

Then I heard something, and I held my breath. The sound came from downstairs, the living room, maybe. It was an unusual sound. A really *weird* sound, as a matter of fact. What *was* that?

Snip—snip—snip...

It sounded like some kind of ... scissors ...

Suddenly something rolled across the foyer at the bottom of the stairs. A ball, no—a head! I stifled a scream.

Then I saw who it was.

My bear! John had decapitated my stuffed bear!

How could he? How DARE he?! Now he was *really* pissing me off!

With new resolve, I moved forward toward my enemy ... but then I heard the sound again.

Snip—snip—snip...

Now what?

Scraps of fabric flew through the air.

I crouched low and peered through the stair railings. He wouldn't ...

He would! I recognized the pattern on that fabric.

How sick!

John was slicing up my new curtains with garden shears!

His voice rang out in maniacal glee: "Now"–*snip!*–"we don't need"–*snip!*–"to get a new rug!" *Snip! Snip!*

I was up and moving like a Trojan warrior, firing shots through the living-room wall, showering my interior *un*decorator with shrapnel.

"Jaaane!" he shouted. "You complete me!"

He was insane, that man; he'd finally lost his fucking mind.

Furious about the curtains, I raced down the stairs, gun first. Just as I turned the corner–

Wham!

A table lamp swung around the corner and hit me, hard!

Stunned, I reached for the wall to brace myself. I couldn't believe it! He'd struck me with a goddamn table lamp!

Didn't he *know* how much that thing cost?

Before I could recover, John lunged out and grabbed for my gun.

We struggled, wrestling, fighting for control of the gun, shots firing wildly, bullets eating up the room as we scuffled across the floor.

Finally I elbowed John in the face, and he went down.

As he fell, I cross-drew two handguns like the bad dude in a Clint Eastwood Western.

Now–wise guy–he was gonna *pay for those curtains*!

But just as I cocked the triggers, that sneaky bastard hooked my legs with the lamp cord. As I fell on my ass, the guns skittered away across the floor.

Gasping for air, John and I lunged to opposite corners. I scrambled for the nearest weaponlike object I could find–the golf trophy!

Yes! I hated golf, hated all those hours he'd spent chasing some stupid little ball as an excuse to hang out drinking with his buddies at the club. "Business," he'd said.

I'd give him business! I spun around and faced him with his precious golf trophy raised high above my head.

If looks could kill, the fight would have been over at that very moment. "That *belongs* to the country club!" he shouted. "I'm only custodian for the year!"

Heh, heh, heh. I smiled darkly and brought the trophy crashing down toward his skull.

John grabbed the fireplace poker and used that to block the blow—but at great cost. The tiny little golfer's head broke off. It hit the hardwood floor with a pitiful *clink*.

John roared like a madman.

Trophy head for curtains!!!

Now it was *really* getting down and dirty! We flew at each other like cats and dogs, elbows and knees flying, bones cracking, flesh bruising, in a wild orgy of martial arts.

We were two master killers beating each other senseless, stumbling over furniture, crashing into walls, destroying the rooms we had once cared about . . .

Somewhere in this mission, our battle had changed. This was far more than combat between two agencies whose operatives had crossed into each other's territory. This was about a helluva lot more than trophies and curtains.

Cold-blooded assassination was one thing. But this was a murderous rage as old as the world itself.

I wanted to *fucking kill* my goddamn husband.

And he obviously wanted to *fucking kill* me. His wife.

Like a boxer, I stumbled back into a corner, spotted my gun, lunged for it. Shaking the sweat from my eyes, I brought the gun up, spun around, and came face-to-face with John—and the business end of the other gun.

It was a showdown. The moment of truth.

We stood there mere inches apart, our chests heaving from the fight, our fingers on twin triggers, while the debris of our marriage wafted around us, littering the floor.

Ragged photos. Bits of fabric. Shards of treasured mementos. Furniture, dishes, walls, and floors.

Our life in ruins.

Our eyes locked, and I think in that moment we truly recognized each other for what we were, the way vampires recognize each other as they walk among the living.

We knew in our gut we'd met a fellow professional killer.

And at this close range, we would easily blow each other to kingdom come.

So this was how it all ended, huh? From saving each other's life in the streets of Bogotá—to ending them on Country Club Drive.

We hung there suspended in the moment, in this little catch-22 we'd fought our way into. Unsure of what to do.

If I ran, he'd shoot me in the back. If I fired first, he'd fire going down. And we'd both be dead.

Not even the best screenwriters in Hollywood could write us both out of this one alive.

I'd had standoffs with death many times in my life, and rarely thought about it longer than the time it took to write up my report.

But for the first time ever I faced it with regret. *If only . . . What if . . .*

I studied John closely. His strong stubborn jaw remained defiant even as he stared down death.

And those lips, those traitorous lips. Despite all their lies, I longed to taste them one more time before one of us—or both of us—dived into the Great Oblivion.

John narrowed his eyes at me, and I suddenly feared he'd read my mind. I needed to hide my feelings, because if I faltered, I knew he'd steal the moment to shoot first. And I wasn't sure if I'd answer fire.

But if it had to be one of us, maybe that's what I wanted anyway. To let him take me out. Better than living to see him die.

My hands trembled as John studied my face, his head cocked.

For a long moment the only sound was our tortured breathing. The world seemed to stand still.

I imagined I felt a change in the chemistry between us.

Then all at once John's shoulders relaxed. His gun dipped.

I swallowed hard, confused. "What are you doing?"

His face was inscrutable as he dropped his weapon to his side. "Go ahead," he said softly.

He took one step forward and leaned into my gun, letting the barrel press into his chest.

Trembling, I blinked the sweat from my eyes. "This is a trick!" I spat.

"No trick," he said simply, his eyes boring into mine. "Now tell me," he demanded roughly, "tell me this is *cold . . . hard . . . math.*"

I couldn't move. I looked away.

Then his hand shot out, I thought perhaps to grab my gun.

But instead he wrapped his strong tanned fingers around mine, like a lover showing the way, then cocked the hammer of my gun—the gun I had pointed at his heart.

Jesus Christ! What was he trying to do?

Slowly I raised my eyes to his. I blinked hard, struggling. Trying hard not to break, fighting it with all my heart and soul.

Throat dry, I tried to say it: "This is cold . . . hard . . ."

John pressed closer, and the gun barrel dug deeper into his chest. I could feel his breath on my skin. Could see the pulse beating along his throat, revealing to me the rapid pounding of his heart, a heart I could easily destroy with the tiniest click.

"Math?" he growled.

My finger slid from the trigger. The gun fell from my hand.

I couldn't do it. And I knew I never would.

Terrified, I felt myself falling, falling . . .

Till John caught me in his arms. In a hungry, crushing embrace.

Like a woman starved, I devoured his kiss and let myself be devoured, too.

And I remembered him. I remembered him . . .

Tearing at each other's clothes, we slid to the floor—a floor littered with the composted mementos of our old life.

Each an assassin; each in complete surrender.

JOHN

Damn! Who is this woman, and what has she done with my wife?

JANE

My husband's torn clothes were lying all over the floor. The house was a wreck. I had totally lost control.

Worked for me.

Lying in a tangle of sweaty garments, among the dust and debris, I couldn't remember when I'd last felt this wonderful.

Yes, I could.

That first time.

"Hiya, stranger," I murmured.

He grinned. "Hiya back."

"Not bad."

"Not too bad yourself." He pointed his finger like a gun and ran it down between my breasts, then drew little circles over my heart. "I should've killed you a long time ago."

I raised one eyebrow. "Kill me again," I purred.

With a growl, he pulled me into his arms, and we plunged

into a delicious, lingering kiss, no hurry now, a kiss that said, *We are not dead; and the hours of a lifetime lie before us in all their possibility.*

Then—I couldn't help myself—I started to giggle.

John pulled back and looked at me. "What?"

"I wonder what the neighbors would say if they could see our 'perfect' house now."

John and I looked at each other and then we both burst into stomach-rocking laughter. John got up and pulled me to my feet. With a wild whoop, he spun me around and around in the littered foyer, and I screamed like a kid on an amusement-park ride, the kind that turns you upside down and takes your breath away.

Then John put me down and took me by the hand, and together, leaving the mess we'd made till morning, we climbed the stairs to bed.

Just an ordinary couple, Mr. and Mrs. Smith.

We made love like newlyweds.

And I saw stars.

JOHN

Sometime just before dawn, stomach rumbling, I headed downstairs, into the ruins of our kitchen.

The fridge was pretty empty, the box of cereal full of holes. Even, sadly, the pie was destroyed. But I was used to improvising.

Like in Bogotá.

Whistling softly, I plucked what I needed from the shattered fruit basket, and soon created a fruit salad worthy of room service at the finest hotel.

I glanced up and caught Jane smiling at me from the doorway.

Jeez, she looked beautiful—so soft and touchable. Gone was the Stepford wife, and the trained killer. In their place was Jane. Just a woman.

My wife.

How long had it been since I'd actually looked at her in the morning light? Really looked at her?

We grinned at the absurdity of it all, to be here, together, in the middle of all this chaos.

And then she was in my arms.

For a moment, we simply held each other and I felt like a man who had just bolted up from a nightmare to discover that everything was all right.

It was a new day. And we had the freedom to start all over again.

I mean, when you thought about it, the whole situation was really kind of funny.

"So how's the software business?" I asked as I offered her some fruit.

She grinned and chose some juicy chunks of peach. "Beats me. How's construction?"

I chuckled. "Lordy knows."

She smiled almost shyly, and I felt an overwhelming desire to tell her how stunning she was.

"That left hook of yours?" I said. "A thing of beauty."

"Thanks," she said. "You take it well."

She tiptoed through the twisted cutlery and broken glass, looking for a coffee cup.

Then she turned with a question in her eyes. "Our vacation in Aspen, when you left early?"

Ah, that. "Jean-Luc Gaspard," I admitted.

She shook her head. "Darn. I wanted him."

"The forty-five-minute showers?" I asked.

She shrugged. "Morning briefings."

She slipped slightly on some spilled condiments but caught herself, and laughed out loud. God, she was amazing—so loose and graceful and . . . free.

"You didn't hear me the night the chopper dropped me off for our anniversary dinner?" I asked.

"No."

I was surprised. "No?"

"Percussion grenade," she explained, pointing at her ears. "Temporary hearing loss . . ."

I nodded. Been there, done that.

Jane finally found what was probably the one unbroken coffee mug in the whole house and went to the sink to rinse it out. But halfway there she winced. Then she reached down and pulled out a shard of glass from her foot and laughed.

Laughed in the middle of all this chaos. Just like that day in Bogotá, giggling in her room as shots rang out and the *policía* swarmed the halls.

God, I couldn't take my eyes off her. An overwhelming feeling in my chest compelled me to confess everything to her.

"I'm a little color-blind," I blurted out.

Her eyes widened. But then she smiled and confessed, "I have no feeling in these three fingers."

"Three ribs," I said. "Fractured eye socket. Perforated eardrum . . ."

"Femur. Fibula. Still can't bend my pinkie . . ."

I met her at the sink, this girl of my dreams, my hands dripping with the juice of the fruit.

"This is why you'd never let me get a dog," I said.

She nodded sadly. "Who'd walk him if I got shot?"

I turned on the water to wash my hands. Our fingers touched as she reached over to rinse a trace of blood from her hand.

We were silent a moment, just thinking about it all.

Then she looked up at me. "Ever have trouble sleeping at night?" she asked softly. "You know, after . . . ?"

Should I tell her what I expected she wanted to hear? Or tell her the truth?

I went for the truth. "Nope."

A crooked smile stole across her lips. "Me neither."

And we both laughed.

"Last Christmas, did you leave three frag grenades in the Mercedes?" I asked.

Jane rolled her eyes. "I was wondering where I put those . . ."

I took her hand and led her to the living room, hoping we might still find something we could sit on.

Man, the room was a wreck. Maybe we could just empty the place, start all over again. Like the day we moved in.

Her eyes fell on the image of her new curtains all tattered and torn while my eyes took in those long dark lashes of hers. The sight of them fanning out on her flushed cheeks made my heart race.

And I wondered what else was going on behind that drop-dead gorgeous face of hers.

A phrase I'd later regret thinking.

Within seconds a red dot appeared on her smooth forehead. Not a smudge. Not any kind of makeup. But a tiny dot of light.

For a moment, out of context, I struggled to make sense of what I was seeing.

Then a green dot appeared on the wall.

Lucky for us both, experience kicked in.

Laser target beams.

Shit!

Some kick-ass long-range gun was aimed right into the center of her brain.

"DOWN!" I screamed as I lunged at her, rolling her back toward the kitchen.

Pffft-pffft-pffft-pffft!

A smoke bomb smashed through the window and erupted on the living-room floor. Bullets strafed the wall above us. If I had hesitated a single second longer, Jane's brains would have been splattered across the wall.

I touched her lovely face, just to reassure myself it was still in one piece.

Drive-by shootings were pretty rare in this neighborhood. Jane's eyes told me she knew what I knew.

Mr. and Mrs. Smith were under attack.

JANE

Red and green laser sight beams crisscrossed above us like holiday lights. But I didn't think they were bringing us tidings of good cheer.

Wham! The front door slammed open, and a dozen shadows pounded across the hardwood floors into the house, not even stopping to wipe their feet.

John and I raced for the French doors that led out back, but the bullets smashing through the glass panes changed our minds. More shadows—incoming from the backyard.

We were surrounded. Even worse, our guns lay spent on the living-room floor.

John pulled me away, whispering, "Follow me! Downstairs!"

I silenced him with a raised finger, then spoke to him in crisp emphatic Navy SEAL hand signals:

NO. TRAPPED. BAD, I motioned.

YES, he signed back. *LISTEN. ME. DOWN. GO!*

NO. IDIOT. THINK, I replied.

John pushed forward toward the basement stairs, dragging me with him.

Then I remembered.

WAIT! I signed. *GUNS. KITCHEN. MINE.*

NO! he signed back. *DANGER. THERE!*

SHUT. UP. AND. LISTEN. ONCE.

I glared. He glared back.

NO. YOU. SHUT. UP. FOLLOW.

FUCK OFF! I gestured. Not a signal you're likely to find in the Navy SEAL handbook, but he got the message.

At that point, we heard footsteps coming our way—no more time to argue.

John shoved me ahead of him down the stairs.

The place was dark and a bit musty, but well organized, thanks to yours truly. Piles of boxes lined the walls, neatly packed, neatly stacked, and alphabetized.

Okay, so maybe it was a bit much, but on this occasion, it just might save our asses.

I quickly scanned them. *A, B, C* . . . CHRISTMAS ORNAMENTS, COLLEGE YEARBOOKS . . . FRATERNITY PARAPHERNALIA, *GOURMET* MAGAZINE . . .

I dragged a box from the top and tore off the lid: It was filled with old but neatly folded winter clothes. Not the latest style, perhaps, but a definite improvement over the near-naked state we found ourselves in. We pulled on shirts, pants, boots—whatever we could find that would fit.

It was the first chance we'd had to catch our breath, to figure out what was going on.

"Jesus! Where's the trust?" John said, yanking on some old pants. "They couldn't've waited a day?"

"We're off the reservation," I said, struggling to button up a man's flannel shirt. Why *did* men wear their buttons on the wrong side? "They gotta send people."

John scanned the boxes, then pulled down one marked MODEL TRAINS and ripped it open. Inside were two weapons—one big, one small. He grabbed the big gun and measured its weight in his hands.

I jammed my fists on my hips. "Why do I get the girl gun?"

"Shhh!"

"But—"

He shoved the big gun into my hands to shut me up, then pointed toward the ceiling.

Footsteps overhead.

Then, before we could move—

BAM! BAM! BAM! Gunfire blasted the basement door off its hinges. A dark silhouette stood at the top of the stairs. "Good night, Ozzie and Harriet," he called down.

Then he dropped something and stepped away. Whatever it was bounced down the stairs. Two small objects rolled across the floor.

Holy shit! His-and-her grenades!

With no time to strategize, John simply kicked them. They looked like toylike objects but clearly they weren't. They rolled across the floor and wedged beneath the water heater.

John shot me a look that said, *Oops.*

I shot him a look that said, *I fucking told you so!*

We were trapped in the basement with a couple of grenades about to explode under the water heater.

Only one option: John grabbed my hand and dragged me toward the basement door.

Padlocked.

Now it was my turn to say *Oops.*

"Now, *who* did *that?*" John said.

I had, the night before, when I was trying to keep him out.

Standing back, he leveled his gun and shot off the lock, yanked open the door, just as—

The grenades blew up the heater. And the entire basement with it. The force propelled us, like stuntmen shot out of a cannon, up and out the door, flames licking at our boot heels.

We ran, crawled, *swam*—however the hell we could move—away from the house, till we were forced to stop and rest. Coughing and gasping for breath, we stared back at our house.

The explosion buckled and thundered through all the other rooms like a heat-seeking missile destroying all our secrets, all our lies. An earthquakelike rumble shook the house from its foundation, until the whole structure simply fell apart, crumbling to the ground in a smoldering pit.

Clinging to each other, we gaped at the destruction, the embodiment of our old lives. It was gone forever.

And then we saw something impossible.

"Goddamn son of a fucking bitch," John whispered. But I could only stare.

The black silhouette—the figure from the top of the stairs—appeared to walk right out of the swirling flames and was heading straight for us. He was unstoppable . . .

Oh, my God! *Move!* my trained mind ordered.

I turned to John. "We need a car!"

Our eyes locked.

"The Colemans," he said.

We ran toward the fence that made us good neighbors. I quick-climbed it in a single leap while John scaled it.

Racing to the garage, we peeked inside—all clear. The Colemans' Dodge minivan was ours for the taking.

Even luckier, they'd backed it in. So all we had to do was jump in and drive straight out. What could be easier?

We stormed the van. John opened the driver's-side door, then noticed something on a counter in the corner of the garage: "Hey—he's had my barbecue tongs for *six months!*"

Pissed, but not in much of a position to do anything about it, John leaped inside and unlocked the passenger-side door for me. As I settled into the seat, he went to work hot-wiring the engine.

Hell, I didn't know he could do stuff like that. I sat there and wondered what else didn't we know about each other. "Uh, John . . . ?"

He grunted, intent on his work.

Should I tell him? We'd already dealt with all the major lies. Would one more little one—revealed or concealed—make a difference now?

Just then I had an overwhelming desire to wipe the slate clean, I mean really clean.

Maybe it was the fires of hell we'd just walked through, or the fact that we could both die in the next few minutes that propelled me to confess.

"I was never in the Peace Corps."

"Oh." He stopped and looked over at me, blinking in surprise. "That's . . . gosh, I *loved* that about you . . ."

I knew it; it was a mistake to dig up small lies. "Maybe this is a bad idea. Everybody lies, right?"

John quickly agreed. "Case in point: I didn't go to MIT. It was Notre Dame. Art history."

He kept his head down, still working on the car, as if it was no big deal.

I wrinkled my nose. "Art?"

"Art *history*," he emphasized. "It's reputable . . ."

I turned and stared out the window. College majors, Peace Corps, favorite colors, TV shows . . . there were so many little things to lie about in a marriage. Where would it end? Was *anything* between us real?

I found myself looking at his hairline.

I saw him glance at my chest.

But all these questions were going to be moot if we didn't get the hell out of here fast. John cursed under his breath as the car turned and turned, but wouldn't start.

Maybe it was a sign.

"Did you check the visor?" I asked.

He shot me a look. "Nobody's that obvious."

"John . . ."

"Jaaaane!" he mocked back.

I rolled my eyes. We were running out of time—no time to waste on male ego.

I casually reached up to the sun visor over the steering wheel and flipped it down.

The keys dropped into John's lap.

I had just enough time for another smug "told you so" look before we heard something.

We shared a look, checked our weapons. Then John pressed the remote for the garage door to open.

As the door rose before us, we saw one of our assassins sprint toward the driveway. Standing in the glare of our headlights, he lined up a shot.

I leaned forward to get a closer look. Who were these monsters who kept coming at us like the living dead? I processed his features.

Coat and tie, neatly combed hair, face like a baby. He looked like a Bible salesman.

"Spooky . . ." I murmured.

"Fuckers get younger every year," John muttered.

He turned the key and the engine roared to life. As we peeled out of the garage, John raised his gun and delivered two precise shots. The assassin went down.

John stopped beside him and reached out to retrieve his weapon.

"Floor it!" I shouted.

"Don't annoy Daddy while he's driving," John said through gritted teeth, then he pulled a hell-on-wheels U-ie around the Colemans' mailbox.

BANGBANGBANG!

Bullets peppered the back windows. But John swerved hard just in time! The sound of gunfire faded in the distance as we drove off into the sunrise.

We didn't speak until we were out on the interstate. And suddenly it was quiet. Too quiet.

John turned on the CD player, which filled the van with the eighties sound of Air Supply singing "Making Love Out of Nothing at All."

The Colemans love soft rock.

Ick. Not one of my favorites. I reached to turn it off. Then noticed something really weird.

John was singing along under his breath.

As I watched in amazement, he got louder and louder, until he was singing like some refugee from a *Wayne's World* movie.

By now I had completely turned in my seat, my mouth hanging open in utter astonishment. Who knew Mr. Country Club Golf Trophy was into eighties megabands, too?

It was just one more secret—a sick fetish he'd hidden from me all these years. I reached for the knob to turn it off, but his hand shot out and beat me to it.

"Hey, I like it," he said in a cold steely voice. "Deal with it."

Then he turned it up louder.

I folded my arms and looked out the window.

But after a while—I hate to admit it—I found myself nodding to the beat.

"Eighth-grade prom," I muttered. "Last dance . . ."

I hummed a few bars as we drove on in silence—well, not exactly silence: two stone-cold half-dressed killers listening to golden moldy rock in a minivan with the back windows blown out.

But I could tell something was on his mind. Some confession or complaint was building up in his head—one that he'd never be able to contain. I could tell by the way he was clenching his jaw. Any minute now he was gonna blow.

Suddenly John blurted out: "I never liked your lemon cake!"

"What?!"

"The lemon cake," he said. "I never liked it . . ."

I sat back in my seat and folded my arms. God, he was really trying to hurt me now. But that was okay. I could blow him out of the water on this one. "No problem," I said smugly. "I never made it."

Now it was his turn to be stunned. "What?!"

"Entenmann's," I revealed. "Five ninety-nine. Microwave three minutes on defrost."

John looked overwhelmed. "Wow," he breathed, shaking his head. "Web of lies . . ."

But before we could stun each other with any more revealed truths, John's eyes zeroed in on the rearview mirror. "Shit, we've got company."

The rest of the confessions would have to wait.

JOHN

A sleek black BMW materialized behind us.

Jane and I glanced back as one car became three—pursuing us like aircraft in formation, closing in for the kill.

I admired Jane's reflexes. A lot of women would have gone all goofy on me—crying and shrieking bloody murder.

Instead, Jane calmly grabbed her gun and prepared to *commit* bloody murder.

As the best of eighties rock blasted from the CD

player, Jane climbed into the backseat. Crawling on her belly, she popped down two rows of reclining seats. I glanced in the rearview. She left the last row's seat back up to use as a shield, then pushed all the rest of the junk in the car toward the trunk space, creating a bunker out of picnic baskets, coolers, hockey gear, and golf clubs.

God, I had no idea people hauled their whole lives around in these things.

Then Jane hit a button and the back window began to open automatically, giving her a clear shot. Aiming over the seat back, she fired!

Unfortunately I had to swerve around a slow-moving pickup, sending her shots high and wide.

"Shit, John!" she shouted. "First time behind the wheel? HOLD STEADY!"

Easier said than done. "How the hell do people drive these things?!" I shouted. The minivan had all the cornering finesse of a drunken bull.

"Try the Macy's parking lot the day after Christmas," Jane said.

Then she was crawling up front. "Move over, John," she demanded.

When I hesitated, she grabbed my arm. "I *know* how to drive these things."

I glared at her. I hated it when she bossed me around.

"Yes, dear," I said grudgingly. If she could drive the damn thing, I'd be free to send our pursuers to their final reward—or I should say final punishment.

As I struggled to hold the van steady, we tried to trade positions, which was tricky as hell going full speed.

Jane wound up on my lap, facing me, wedged between

my body and the wheel. Not a bad position for a drive-in movie, but dangerous, in more ways than one, when the car was flying down the interstate at eighty miles an hour.

I shifted uneasily. Her eyes bored into mine. And it felt like staring into the demanding eyes of Saint Peter himself.

We froze for a moment, eyes locked. So many unanswered questions rumbling like thunder between us.

But hell, we didn't have time for this—we had to move.

I squirmed out from under her, and she scooted around to take over the driving. Just in time, too, because she barely had her hands on the wheel when—

Wham! One of the pursuit cars slammed into us, rocking us hard.

Jane adjusted the rearview mirror to her height while I crawled to the gunner's bench at the back of the van.

Back in action, we were two suburban warriors, ready to take on the world.

A blast of heavy machine-gun fire exploded from the cars behind us, chewing up the windows from a rear side of the minivan. The car that rammed us before was back, too, moving up on the passenger side like a shark going in for the kill.

"Incoming!" I yelled. "Your side! Veer left!"

Jane checked my information in her side-view mirror, as if she were changing lanes on her way to the mall.

Damn, another black BMW was speeding up on the driver's side. Didn't she see it?

"Today, preferably!"

I caught the look on her face in the rearview mirror, and she looked mad as hell. Just because

I hadn't handed her any more juicy confessions? God, she just always had to have her way.

"All right, all right!" I yelled. "I was married once. Before."

I wasn't surprised that my confession went over like a ton of bricks. She looked totally broadsided.

"What?"

"Yeah," I said, trying to downplay it. "Thought you should know."

I waited for a reaction, but she just seemed to be digesting the news. Okay. Good.

Then suddenly she stood on the brakes, a full lockdown. She was so angry, I thought her hair was going to catch fire.

But before I could say anything else about it, the car behind us slammed into our rear, its hood jamming under the minivan, lifting our back wheels completely off the road. We were piggybacking down the highway at ninety miles an hour!

Damn! I was flung against the dash. My gun forced from my hand. Golf clubs assailed me from the back. Fighting to dodge them, I somehow wound up in a crumpled ball between the front seats.

Jane glared down at me. I tried to smile, knowing full well that this was one lie I probably should have left buried forever.

"It was five minutes," I protested. "It was no big deal."

"No big DEAL?" she exclaimed.

"It was just a Vegas thing," I said.

Jane's response was to start punching the living daylights out of me.

"Stop it. Stop it!" I gestured with a golf club. "I mean it."

We didn't have time for this! We had to kill these guys who were trying to kill us. *Then* Jane and I could kill each other.

I rolled toward the rear, golf club in hand. Then crawled out the back hatch and onto the hood of the pursuing BMW.

An assassin popped up out of the car's sunroof. But I was armed and ready. Before he could take aim, I clubbed him across the head with a one wood.

I had *told* Jane all those hours on the golf course would pay off.

As the assassin fell back across the roof, I noticed a grenade attached to his vest. Thinking fast, I reached over and pulled the pin, shoved the man into the car, then dove back into the minivan.

"Floor it, Jane! Go! Go!"

Jane must have heard the urgency in my voice, because for once she didn't hesitate. She stomped the gas, our front-wheel drive kicked in, and we pulled away from the piggybacked car just as—

Blam! It exploded in an earth-shattering fireball.

"Well done," Jane called from the front.

"Thanks, hon," I called back.

As our remaining windows shattered, I lay facedown in the rear.

Jane didn't speak for a moment. But I could tell by the way she didn't that she was gonna.

"What's her name?" Jane demanded at last. "Social Security number?"

Yeah, right. Like I was going to tell her. "No, no, you'll just go kill her. And she was nice." Jane shot me a look that would freak the devil. "Uh, I mean, not *too* nice . . ."

Pissed, Jane took it out on the only thing at hand.
The assassins.

The two remaining cars formed a Jane sandwich by
moving up on either side of our van.

No-fear Jane veered hard into the car on the left.

Ka-POOF! The side-impact air bag inflated, cata-
pulting me clear across to the other side of the van.

Meanwhile, Jane slammed into the other car like a
tank, shoving it across two lanes, through a break in
the median straight into oncoming traffic.

As the other sedan followed, I tried to get on my
feet so I could take aim.

But Jane swerved sharply back across the highway,
now slamming the second car into the concrete di-
viders. When the other air bag blew, I was tossed,
once again, to the other side of the car like a rag
doll.

Sparks flew as Jane continued to put the pedal to
the metal. With the second car still pinned to the
median, she was scraping paint at a speed nearly
twice the legal limit!

"What?" I said as I opened the side door. "You were
a Girl Scout? You never told a big one?"

Jane looked away.

Okay, no news is bad news. But lucky her, before I
could grill *her*, we looked through the windshield and
saw a big rig bearing down on us. Head-on!

"Shit!" Jane shouted. "Hang on!"

She yanked the wheel hard, and the eighteen-wheeler
roared by—so close it shaved the top layer of paint
off our van.

But while we were distracted, yet another BMW full
of assassins moved up alongside us.

"Incoming!" Jane shouted. "Three o'clock!"

"Your three o'clock or my three o'clock?" I hollered. "See, this is what I'm trying to tell you . . . Communication is the key."

"Oh, for God's sake!" Jane exclaimed. She pointed at the operative jumping from his car as he opened the sliding door on her side of the van.

With one push I sent him careening through the passenger door all the way on the other side of the van.

"God, these doors are handy!" I said.

The remaining assassins, undeterred by one of their own turned into roadkill, didn't even slow down. Instead they swerved toward us, smashing us back into no-man's-land—and straight for some of those pesky yellow barrels.

At the last second Jane smashed into our foes, sending them through the barrels and out onto the wrong side of the highway.

I quickly closed both side doors, and locked them this time. We'd had enough drop-in guests for one day.

Finally, we had a brief moment of calm.

I know, I know, I shoulda just used it to catch my breath. But you know how it is when something's bugging you.

"Truth, Jane. Your parents never liked me, did they?"

Jane paused, then said, "My parents are dead."

"What?!" I felt like I'd taken a direct hit.

"They died when I was five," Jane confessed. "I barely remember them."

I blinked at her in disbelief. Totally wounded by this ultimate deception.

"Happy now?" she snapped. "Jane's an orphan."

I was completely floored.

I just sat there with my damn mouth hanging open, staring at the stranger beside me. This last confession—it was too much. Lines had been crossed. I felt completely unmoored.

She had no parents. No mother, no father . . .

"Then who is that guy I play golf with every Sunday?" I shouted.

Jane had enough conscience to flinch. "An actor," she said.

An actor?! Was she *kidding*? Christ! That was the most devious thing I'd ever heard of! I couldn't believe it. And yet—now it all made sense. *That's* why he'd always seemed so familiar. I pounded the dashboard. "I *said* I saw your dad on *Fantasy Island*!"

For a moment the inside of the van was quiet. Air Supply was heading for a major crescendo.

And I was reeling from . . . well, everything. I was hurt, really hurt.

To be honest, I guess Jane was, too.

Quietly, through my clenched teeth, I ground out, "We're gonna have to redo every conversation we've ever had."

Jane nodded solemnly. "Yeah, I know . . ."

We looked at each other, daunted by the morning-after reality of our life together. Our sham of a marriage. Collapsing like a house of cards.

Could a marriage possibly hold this many lies—and survive?

Then I saw that the black BMW brigade hadn't really given up; they'd only been preparing for their final assault.

I went into autopilot and did what I had to do as the two sedans split up to flank us.

"I got 'em, Jane. I got 'em."

I crouched low, my back against the front seats as I waited for the attack. Like a hero in an old Western, this was the last stand.

Then I hit the buttons. Both doors began to open. The cars moved closer and closer. My head swiveled back and forth as I checked out both sides, waiting for my perfect moment.

The cars nosed into range . . .

Suddenly—*wham!* Jane jerked the steering wheel, sending the minivan into a hundred-and-eighty-degree spin.

Crap! Unprepared, I was thrown across the floor, my fingers grabbing for anything I could hold on to but finding only smooth surfaces instead as I slid out the door!

I was barely hanging on to the side of the minivan. In fact, I was struggling to crawl back inside, fighting impossible g-force and trying unsuccessfully to figure out what in *hell* my wife was doing when suddenly I realized the van had swung all the way around. We were now speeding a hundred miles an hour in REVERSE—actually FACING the cars that were chasing us.

An insane maneuver—but I was too busy hanging on to actually voice my opinion on the matter.

Not that Jane would have paid much attention to my opinion right now anyway.

I watched, amazed, as she precision-fired, automatic shots at the first car's bulletproof windows. This time, the bullets penetrated them, shattering the glass.

The driver was instantly killed.

Then she repeated the attack on the second car—with the same results.

The sedans spun out of control, crashing into each

other as they continued to speed down the highway.

I managed to pull myself back into the van and watch in amazement as the cars pinballed behind us.

Then, without warning—*wham!* Like a racecar driver on speed, Jane spun the minivan, and I was airborne once again.

This time I managed to stay inside.

Seconds later, we were back on track, going a hundred miles an hour in the FORWARD position.

Fucking unbelievable.

I crawled to the front and dropped into the passenger seat.

And I was pissed. "I told you I *had* that!"

She glanced sideways. "Whoops."

Sarcastic, of course.

As we drove away from the flaming wreckage in our battered but unbeaten Road Warrior van, Air Supply brought the eighties to a dramatic close.

We'd made it through this episode alive.

Now what?

I sank into my seat and glared out my window. I knew I was acting like a sulky child. But hell, that's how I felt.

JANE

So. We'd made it through that episode alive. But I wasn't sure whether it was because of—or in spite of—our teamwork.

And now what?

So many lies. His marriage, my parents . . . how could we ever survive?

Last night I thought we'd found each other again. But this

morning, as reality poured in, I just didn't know anymore.

Sometimes things were so broken, they just couldn't be repaired.

John and I looked at each other, then turned toward the road ahead.

"Any thoughts on breakfast?" I asked.

He shrugged. "Left my wallet at home."

"We can go back," I suggested.

He looked at me, then sadly shook his head.

Yeah, I didn't think so, either.

JOHN

When I showed up at the diner, Eddie was so busy scarfing down his usual all-you-can-eat breakfast he didn't even notice me.

Finally, looking up to check out the waitress's ass, he saw me. "John!" he cried. "Jesus, thank God!"

"Morning, Eddie."

He grabbed my arm. "Please tell me: Did you kill the bitch?"

I signaled to Eddie that we had company.

Sitting on the stool beyond me, Jane gave Eddie a nicer smile than he deserved.

I think it was the first time I'd ever seen Eddie blush.

"Let me rephrase that," he muttered.

But Jane cut to the chase. "Eddie, we've got problems."

Eddie snorted. "No, no. Crack addicts have problems. You two are—how do I put this?" He waved a hand in the air, as if trying to find the words to describe a fine wine. "You're *fucked*!"

Great. Not what I was hoping to hear. "Maybe," I said.

"Maybe?" Eddie exclaimed. "You have all of our agency gunning for you. And probably all of hers, too!"

"But not you," I pointed out.

Eddie shook his head and turned back to his heart-attack special. "I'm dragging my feet this morning, if you know what I mean. For old time's sake." He grunted. "And you owe me money, I think."

The waitress stopped by, a big smile wrapped around her wad of gum. "You folks ordering?"

"Yeah, I'll take some waffles, butter on the side, and half a grapefruit," I said. "And an order of wheat toast for the missus."

"Dry, please," Jane added.

Eddie held out his cup. "And could I get some more—" But the waitress had moved on. Guess she was familiar with Eddie's tipping history.

Jane slipped her hand into mine—a soft, quiet gesture—and for the first time I noticed she was still wearing her ring. My chest seemed too tight all of a sudden.

I turned back to Eddie. "I don't suppose there's any hope we apologize, they give us our jobs back."

"If she works for who the street says she works for—" He looked at Jane for confirmation.

She confirmed with a nod.

"—then you're Coke and she's Pepsi. Macy's and Gimbel's. The WE channel and whatever the hell channel hates the WE channel." He shook his head, his face grim. "Once you're off the reservation, you're *off* the reservation."

"So we run," Jane said simply.

It was one of the options I'd considered. But easier said than done in our world. "What are our
chances, you think?"

"On your own?" Eddie mopped up the last of his egg
with his toast, then stuffed it into his mouth. "I'd
give ten-to-one odds you survive. Together?" He shook
his head. "A hundred-to-one."

That bad? I cursed under my breath. Eddie was kind
of a pig when it came to food, but I trusted his judg-
ment when it came to most everything else.

"Hey," he said, not unkindly, burping as he leaned
back from the counter. "There's a reason God made the
no-fault divorce."

Jane and I let the words sink in. Suddenly I wasn't
very hungry. We canceled our order, left a tip anyway, and headed outside.

I stuffed my hands in my pockets as we slowly
drifted outside onto the street. We came to a stop in
the parking lot.

I waited for her to leave. I guess I wanted a last
look or something. But she just stood there, waiting
for me to leave first.

What the hell were we supposed to do? The whole
fucking world seemed against us. We were putting each
other in danger just standing on the same block together.

We looked at each other. One final time.

Then . . . we found ourselves crossing the street.
Together. Toward a Verizon van.

Something was keeping us connected. Hell if I knew
what it was.

Hell if I cared, either.

But we figured we were in this together. At least
for now. And now was all we had.

"What we need is something we can trade for our lives," I said.

Jane was right there with me. "Something they want *more* than they want us dead."

Damn, I could almost see the computer working inside of her pretty little head, surfing the World Wide Web of her mind.

And then she smiled. Like a cat.

She'd found the answer.

"What . . . ?"

She told me her idea.

Damn! She had a plan, and the guts to pull it off. I didn't want to like it. I didn't want to admire her. But it was a good idea.

Jeez, if we had ten minutes to spare . . .

But time was of the essence, like she'd said. Every second we waited was another second one of our teams could put a bullet through our heads.

So. Our plan?

We were going after Benjamin Danz.

You remember him—he was the bastard we were both after when we first almost killed each other, back in that blazing hot desert. Everybody wanted this guy—our team, her team, the FBI. Why? We had no fucking idea. But we knew that if we could get our hands on him, then maybe we could bargain our way out of this hellhole of a situation.

Apparently, the FBI had him down at the federal courthouse.

Jane said it would be easy. Like picking up pork chops at the market.

Damn, did I mention I love this babe?

JANE

$\mathcal{I}$ guess it was just one of those pivotal spur-of-the-moment decisions. One minute Eddie was telling us we didn't have a ghost of a chance.

And the next minute, John and I are driving away together, betting our lives on a crazy plan.

I glanced at him. Something kept holding us together.

Did he feel it, too?

Maybe there was still something good between us—something worth saving.

Or maybe we were like drunks who couldn't keep their hands off the very thing that was poisoning them.

I shivered and turned my mind back to our scheme. We had a big job to pull off.

And then—if we survived—maybe we'd have the chance to figure out the rest of the madness.

JOHN

So there we were that night, setting up the mission in a beat-up van parked outside the courthouse. I was gearing up—prepping our guns, strapping on a minicam head unit—while Jane tuned up her surveillance operation.

She really looked hot when she was working. No wonder she'd been so successful in this business. She had an unfair advantage! Hell, she had probably had guys crawling on their hands and knees . . .

Okay. I was *definitely* not liking the images flooding my mind.

"Can I ask you a question?" I blurted.

She nodded absently, double-checking a reading.

I cleared my throat. "How many?"

She glanced at me, head cocked, obviously puzzled. Then her eyes widened when she realized what I was asking.

"It's that important to you?"

Well, not really, but . . . *yeah! Hell, yeah, it was.*

"Just give me a number," I said casually. "I won't ask anything else. So . . . how many?"

Jane looked away. Hell, maybe I was being a jerk. I didn't mean to make her uncomfortable. But, damn. I really needed to know.

"You want me to go first?" I asked.

Jane sighed. "O-kay."

"I don't exactly keep count," I began, trying not to sound conceited, "but . . . well, I'd say be-tween . . . fifty and sixty."

She bit her lip, absorbing the news. Poor kid. I knew it was probably a shock.

"Sorry if that sounds bad," I hurried to say. "I've been around the block."

I looked at her expectantly.

She hesitated, then shrugged. "Three hundred and twelve."

"*What?!*" I shrieked.

Jane winced. "I shouldn't have told you." Then: "Some of them were two at a time," she tried to ex-plain.

As if that made it all right!

"Are you *counting* innocent bystanders?" I exclaimed.

She glared at me, insulted that I would even sug-gest that.

I just sat there, digesting the news. I was trying not to act like a baby about it, but *damn! That was a lot of hits!*

Something beeped on one of the monitors, but I barely noticed. Jane had to give me a shove.

"Baby's in the crib," she reported, all business now. "You ready?"

I nodded, strapped on the last of my equipment, and climbed out of the van.

"Three hundred and twelve!" I muttered, and slammed the door behind me.

JANE

I loved this part.

Yes, it's always fun to go in and perform—the athletics, the acting, the chase, the escape.

But sitting here in the ops van was so cool—like being in *Star Wars,* or having the newest video game or gadget that no one else had.

I did get a thrill from being in control.

Outside, the van looked like a refugee from a cheap Hollywood used-car lot. Inside, it looked like mission control for a moon landing. I was surrounded by monitors that fed me information: a schematic of the building, alarm systems. Plus, I could see everything from John's POV via the minicam he wore strapped to his forehead: all of the thrills, none of the spills.

As John penetrated the building, I typed in info, checked readings, monitored movement inside—I could see things John couldn't see and tell him what to do, where to go, what to avoid. It didn't hurt that I could type at the speed of light. Without typos.

I typed furiously—alarm systems went down.

More typing—security systems crashed.

Monitor check: John was crawling through the airshafts; not much interesting to see yet.

But just wait.

With our communications system, John could speak quietly into a body mike, and I could hear everything he said through my earpiece.

"You check the perimeter?" he asked as he crawled.

"I checked the perimeter."

"You on the police bands?"

"I'm on the police bands."

"Are you—"

"Hey," I said, a little irritated. "This is *not* my first time."

"Don't remind me."

Smart-ass!

John kept moving, his flashlight striking the walls. I checked his position on the schematic of the airshafts. "Okay: John, turn left."

He wasn't turning left.

"John? Turn *left!*"

Suddenly the image from his minicam began to shake and tumble, as if he were falling—or as if someone had ripped the equipment from his head.

What was happening?

And then John's face filled the screen—his flashlight pointed up from the base of his chin, creating a strange interplay of light and shadow that made him look like a demon.

"Don't tell me what to doooo . . ." he said in a deep scary voice.

He must have been a real scream on Halloween.

His antics reminded me: I was used to working with an all-female crew, but John was—very obviously—a guy. One of my favorite things about him, actually.

I could forget about being in control.

Fortunately he slipped the cam back on and turned into an adult again.

Soon he'd reached a pivotal location.

"Okay, okay, you're there, you're there," I instructed. "Hold here . . ." More typing. "On my mark, proceed–"

The monitor showed me that he was already moving forward.

What the hell was he doing?

"John? . . . *John!* On my *mark!*"

An alarm rang in my headpiece. *Shit!* On the live feed– running! Bedlam!

I typed more furiously "*Dammit, John!*"

And then all the lights went out.

I heard shouting, stumbling. And suddenly–

BAROOM! John had successfully set off his explosives. I could hear a wall coming down. Heard people–guards?–stumbling about, coughing as gas filled the chamber.

Over my headphones I heard a man shout, "Can I get a gun?"

"Shut up!"

"Hey! *Uncuff me!*"

"*Zip it!*"

A prisoner and guards, sounded like. Benjamin Danz?

I listened closely for telltale signs.

Thud. Thud . . . Thud. Bodies hitting the ground. The gas doing its job.

John's gas mask would help him keep his head while all those around him were losing theirs. Things were going well. It wouldn't be long now.

John was damn good at what he did; hadn't I seen him in action, up close and personal? Still . . .

This was the hard part of sitting in the van.

The waiting . . .

Minutes later I saw a hunchbacked figure darting toward the van–John with a body across his shoulders.

Let's hope he'd grabbed the right one in all the confusion.

I opened the side door and met Benjamin Danz for the first time as John thrust him into the backseat. It was him all right, I recognized him from our photos; I never forget a face. His hands were still tied, and the sprint through the fresh night air had quickly counteracted the effects of the gas. He was starting to come to.

John climbed in, ripping equipment off his head and body. Thank God; he was safe.

I tore out of there at lightning speed.

But now that I knew he was alive—I was gonna *kill* him!

"I told you to wait for my signal!" I yelled over my shoulder. "Did you wait for my signal?"

"Yeah, yeah, but I got worried I might turn *sixty* before you gave it!" he shouted back.

"Well, yes, you do *move* like a geriatric!"

"God—do you have to control *everything*!?" John exclaimed. "Ninety percent of this job is instinct!"

"You deviated from the plan!" I reminded him. "Your *instinct* set off every alarm in the building!" I hit the steering wheel in frustration. "Ooh! This is so typical!"

"What, *what*?"

"We sit down, we talk something out, we agree on a plan. Then you completely ignore it!"

"Because *you* never take what *I* want into account!" John shouted. "It's always the Jane show!"

The Jane show! "That's because I've seen the *John* show," I yelled. "It's all half-assed!"

He started to protest, but I cut him off. "My mother's birthday party when *someone* forgot to bring the gift?!"

"Your *fake* mother's birthday party?!"

In the rearview mirror, he looked like he was about to have a stroke.

"I really don't see how this marriage is ever going to work!" John muttered.

And at last Benjamin Danz spoke.

"WHO THE FUCK *ARE* YOU PEOPLE?!?!"

JOHN

We drove into the night, silent and brooding, for what seemed like hours, out of the city and out into the sticks. But we still had work to do. So as soon as possible, we followed signs down a side road and checked into a dive motel.

We threw Benjamin's coat on over him and snuck him in like he was a buddy who'd had a few too many drinks, not that anybody around this place was likely to notice or care.

Once inside, I tied him to a chair in the center of the room. A lamp stripped of its shade added just the right ambience.

I stood in front of him, stretching out my shoulders from the long ride, shirtsleeves rolled up to show a little muscle. I'd never really done much interrogation work. But I figured it couldn't hurt.

Jane, meanwhile, was pacing the room like a caged cat.

"Okay, are we rolling?" I said.

We'd decided to videotape the kid's confession, just in case.

Okay, we were taping.

I decided to try the direct approach.

"Okay, Ben. Go. Give us what you've got."

Ben stared straight into the videocamera: "Look, Ma. I'm on TV."

Okay, I did not like this dude's attitude. But I tried to keep my cool.

"See, Benjamin, you're our get-out-of-jail-free card. Simple question. Tell us why both our bosses want us dead."

I waited, but Benjamin kept his mouth shut. He even raised his chin. And smirked.

God, I hate to be smirked at.

Now I was getting mad—the dude was embarrassing me in front of my date. I nudged him with my toe. "No? Okay. Now, I realize you witnessed my wife and me working through some domestic issues. That's regrettable. But I don't want you to see that as a sign of weakness. It would be a mistake on your part." I glanced at my wife. "Right, Jane?"

Jane stared at me like I'd grown horns. "What do you think you're doing, John?"

I frowned. "You know, honey. Maybe it's not such a good idea for you to undermine me in front of our hostage. Sends a mixed message."

Jane scowled. "If this is anything like the way you load the dishwasher—"

"Please. *Jane.* I have a system here, and I'm implementing it. You've never seen me at work."

Furious, Jane turned her back on me with a dismissive wave. But I was not going to let her competitiveness ruin my work.

I turned back to our captive. He was all but laughing at me now. But I'd soon wipe that smile off his face. "All right, Benjy. Let me lay out your options.

"Option A: You talk, I listen. Pain-free. Option B: You clam up, I remove your fingernails with my jumper cables. Option C?" I tried for a sinister smile. "I like to vary the details, but bottom line: You end up in a body bag."

Ben's smile said: *Fuck you!* But I saw that he was

looking a little shaky. "Could I get a soda or something? I'm a little thirsty—" I heard a noise behind me. And before either of us knew what was happening, Jane flew out of nowhere and slammed a phone into Benjamin's mouth.

"A! A!" Danz shouted through bloody lips. "Option A!"

Jane glanced at me, a smug smile on her face that said, *See? That's all it took.*

But then I noticed Danz jerking strangely, his head bent at an odd angle toward his shoulder.

"What is that?" I asked. "A seizure?"

"My pocket," Danz gasped. "Check my pocket."

Jane and I exchanged a look, then she went over and dug around in his back pockets.

I guess I was expecting a weapon of some sort, so I was surprised when Jane pulled out a photo.

Doubly shocked when I saw that it was a picture of two people near and dear to my heart.

Me and Jane. Together. Shopping.

What the hell—!

"I'm not the target," Benjamin blurted out. "*You* are. Both of you."

I felt like a linebacker had just slammed into my chest. All the air seemed to be sucked out of the room.

Jane looked speechless, too. Which was saying a lot.

"They found out you were married," Benjamin revealed. "So they teamed up and sent you to the same spot . . . to target *each other*."

Now it was all making sense. *Top priority. Direct threat to the firm,* Atlanta had said. *Need your expertise.*

rest of Danz's clothes, looking for the bug. Nothing, dammit, nothing. Where was it?

Then my eyes fell on his belt buckle.

I ripped the strap out of the loops, then popped open the buckle casing.

Bingo.

Inside was a tiny microtransmitter.

And if I were a betting man—which I am—I'd bet that tiny bug was tattling to Atlanta and Father right at this very moment, informing them of our exact location.

With a muttered curse, I turned the transmitter off.

But I guess it was too late. The choppers were still coming our way.

Damn. "Two minutes," I said to Jane.

As she stood at the window, Jane's face went pale. *"One."*

I quickly joined her and looked up into the sky.

Six black choppers in attack formation were heading straight for the motel.

JANE

Gut instinct and a dose of adrenaline got us out of there just in time.

But Atlanta's and Father's gofers would be swarming after us within minutes.

So John and I pounded through the deserted parking garage where we had left our van, trying to come up with a plan as we ran.

John yanked open the driver's-side door.

But I hesitated—trying desperately to think beyond the next ten minutes.

Yeah, right.

They'd sent us both to the same hit—hoping only one of us would come home.

I could tell Jane had worked the same puzzle and come up with the same answer that I had.

"So," Jane said, "you were just . . ."

"Bait." Benjamin shrugged, kind of embarrassed to be doing such a weaselly job. "It's entry level. Toehold in the company. Couple hits, they bump me upstairs to a desk."

Jane stared at the picture.

I glared at Benjy boy.

What a loser. I should have known as soon as I saw his face back in my office that he was a total joke. "The Tank," my ass!

And I couldn't believe he was carrying incriminating, photographic evidence around on his person. Even a beginner knows better than that. "You kept this in your pocket?" I exclaimed.

"What'd you want me to do?" Danz said sarcastically. "Frame it?"

"Burn it," I shot back. "Ditch it. Tradecraft 101."

"Yeah, sorry," Benjamin replied. "Guess I skipped class that day. Maybe *you* skipped the day about *not marrying the enemy!* What's that?" He sneered. "Advanced tradecraft?"

I saw Jane cock her head, listening. The wheels were turning in her head. What . . . ?

"Ben," Jane said sharply. "You *were* bait . . . you *are* bait . . . ?"

Our eyes locked. Now I heard . . .

A sound we both were all too familiar with.

CHOPPERS—*INCOMING!*

Jane ran to the window while I pawed throu

"John," I said, stopping him. "My out's a double-blind ticket to a boat moored in La Paz."

John blanched, then looked away a moment, his jaw clenched. "Mine's a cargo drop in the Atlas Mountains," he said at last.

Then he just looked at me. Like I was some kind of traitor.

But what the hell did he expect? This whole relationship of ours was a total disaster—the marriage, the job. We had to face reality. We'd be insane even to consider staying together.

"Apart, at least we know what the odds are," I argued. "Together . . ." I shrugged.

But still he said nothing.

Damn him! He wasn't making this any easier! "Let's call this what it is finally . . ."

I crossed to the other side of the car and, for old time's sake, handed him my spare ammo.

Then I turned to leave.

"You're a fucking idiot."

His words echoed in the empty garage.

I whirled back around, about to spit fire, when he threw a hard right punch at my jaw! I couldn't believe it!

The cad!

But even surprised, I blocked the punch brilliantly and shot back a reply.

That's all it took. Every crazy emotion we'd lived through over these past few days finally erupted into one angry melee. We fell upon each other—fighting, kicking, punching . . . and blocking every blow.

We were so perfectly matched, so equally trained and experienced, we could have fought like that for hours with no one emerging as the victor.

At last, we found ourselves in each other's arms again—a sweaty body lock, our faces inches apart.

"Really?" John said. "We're gonna do this again?"

I glared at him but couldn't find the words to express what I was feeling.

"Okay," he growled, "it's a crap marriage! I don't know you—you don't know me. I'm a liar—you're a liar. We're *all* liars."

I didn't want to hear this. I fought in his arms, but this time he held me close. Too close.

"Jane," he said. "Let's see this thing through." His voice was a command, but his eyes begged in a way that nearly broke my heart. "Then," he went on, "if you want to go . . . I won't stop you."

I glared at him, struggling to resist. I didn't want to do this. I *couldn't!* If I left now, I could still get out of this alive. But if I stayed, and hoped . . .

Well, this time, if it crashed and burned, I didn't know if I could survive.

And I wasn't talking about the job.

Run, Jane! my heart warned. *Now! Get the hell out of town while you've still got the chance!*

Jane . . . ? Jane!

But John's eyes pleaded.

"Fine," I snapped, trying to hold on to my anger—and my dignity—as my heart caved. "But I'm driving."

"Fine," John fired back.

Without another word, we climbed into the van.

I prayed I hadn't taken the wrong turn.

Our plan was simply brilliant. Or brilliantly simple.

Either way, it was all we had to go on.

Our next stop: one of John's favorite Chinese places. No, not a restaurant—a laundry service.

Who wouldn't want to change into a clean shirt? I thought. This Bonnie-and-Clyde stuff was getting old.

But there was more to it than that. With a smug smile, John

pulled out a weathered ticket and handed it to Madam Wu, the woman who ran the place. She studied the ancient stub with a frown, then silently retreated to the back room.

A few minutes later several of her workers emerged with a large bag, which they dropped to the counter with a surprisingly heavy *clunk*.

I covered my mouth to keep from laughing. John's shirts rattled like metal. Too much starch perhaps?

"Very heavy shirts," Madame Wu grunted.

John smiled. "Very heavy."

We grabbed the bags and ran.

As we jumped into the van, John tossed the bags into the back, then turned around and winked at me.

I couldn't help myself. I blew him a kiss in return.

Then I started up the van and drove me and my partner toward our own personal High Noon.

Partner . . . As we sped toward our mission, I took a moment to think about this man—this stranger—I'd called my husband for six long years. So what if his taste in music left little to be desired?

He was strong. Sharp under fire. An experienced professional with intelligence, expertise, and courage. Not to mention gifted in many leisure-time activities.

I hated to admit it, but we were two of a kind, John and I. How could we have gone for six long years without seeing it in each other?

And the plan? It was insane, of course.

But so was life.

Together, John and I just might make the whole thing work.

JOHN

Ah, kisses. Just one of the things Jane was good at blowing.

As I watched her throw the van into reverse, I wondered if there was a law against having this much fun with your wife. You heard me.

Screw the danger, screw the fates—being on the run with Jane was more fun than I'd had in a long, long time.

This woman—this stranger I'd called my wife for five years—was a total surprise package.

She was smart, braver than most men, and a talented professional with remarkable skill. Not to mention beautiful and sexy as all hell.

We were two of a kind. Yet we'd both been too blind to notice.

Hell, maybe we'd thrown it all away. But maybe, just maybe . . .

I struggled to stop my thoughts there. I had to stay focused on the job at hand. Our plan was pretty damn crazy, but if we could pull it off, I might have many happy days and nights to spend with this woman I called Mrs. Smith.

In fact, I think we'd be due a vacation.

Maybe even a second honeymoon.

JANE

We've all done the "shop till you drop" thing.

You might call what John and I planned to do "shop till you drop . . . dead."

I just had to make damn sure we weren't the ones who died in the end.

We were just outside of our delivery point: HomeMade, my favorite home-furnishings superstore. It seemed the perfect place to start our new life.

John and I had pulled into the parking lot early, just another young couple shopping to furnish their apartment with great things at modest prices. But as far as we knew, we were the only couple going in wearing his-and-her bulletproof Kevlar undies. Not the most comfortable shopping clothes, but if all went well, we'd be spending the next few weeks in as few clothes as possible.

Drunk on love and possibilities, we had been giddy throughout the planning. We hoped to soon be free. Free to live our lives like we wanted. Together.

But now reality was sobering us. As if by some sort of unspoken agreement, we geared up for our mission in silence, careful to avoid touching. We were highly trained, experienced, kick-ass assassins psyching up for our next assignment.

Like Olympic athletes, we needed to be in the zone.

Hard for me, though. No ordinary assignment had ever meant so much. In the past, most of my skill and courage came from the fact that I never thought all that much about what I was risking when I put my life on the line. Of course, no one wants to die. But before, my motivation had been a vague survival instinct; now I truly had something to live for.

My life. With John.

Everything I'd ever learned would be put to the test here. The lessons from every bullet I'd ever dodged, from every wound I had ever sustained, and the muscles, reflexes, and cunning I'd honed throughout more than three hundred missions now came together in this one final fight.

We sat in the car, waiting, going over the plan in our minds. And then it was time to go; we'd procrastinated long enough.

Suddenly John reached for me ... but it was only to adjust my body armor. "Your midstrap ballistic panel..." he whispered softly.

The gesture said more to me than a lifetime of candlelit dinners.

As I turned to acknowledge it, I read the fear in his eyes.

We were walking by choice into a helluva situation. We knew the odds were against us. You might even call it suicide.

Each of us had lost sight of the other before—in our beige suburban marriage. But after finding each other anew, was I again about to lose John and he me? Forever?

But what choice did we have?

If we did nothing, they'd find us and kill us anyway. This way we at least had a chance to go out fighting.

And—thanks to John's "laundry"—we had one hell of an arsenal to back up our fight.

We kissed, a soft lingering kiss, refusing to let it mean goodbye. Then I held John's face in my hands for a moment, drinking in his strength, infusing him with the power of my love.

We would hold strong for each other, we pledged with our eyes.

Then I turned my body and mind to my work.

John reached into his pocket and pulled out the microtransmitter from Benjamin Danz's belt. The one that our agencies had used to track us down.

He clicked the tiny chip back into place and instantly a light flashed.

That told me that the transmitter was working again, no doubt instantly tattling our whereabouts to Atlanta and Father.

They'd be here soon.

"Ready, honey?" John asked.

"Born ready, sweetie," I replied.

We headed into the store with a couple of shopping bags, as if we had some returns. But they were really filled with weapons.

John picked up one of those small baskets as if we were only stopping in for one or two items. I rolled my eyes. The guy obviously didn't engage in retail therapy much.

No way was I heading into a home-furnishings store like HomeMade—or a dangerous shoot-out, for that matter—with anything less than a full-size shopping cart. It was a great prop, something to duck behind in a pinch, and a large, bulky weapon on wheels. Plus, I really needed something to haul all these weapons around in—this stuff was heavy!

But more importantly, you never know when you just might find something precious on sale. After all, we'd lost a hell of a lot of stuff when our house blew up.

So I grabbed a cart and made him choose one, too, hiding our weapons in them under a large selection of half-priced sheets and towels.

Then we casually strolled up and down the aisles, pretending to browse, but what we were really shopping for were assassins. The more we looked, the more everybody appeared suspicious.

That guy over in bunk beds. The couple paying for garden furniture. The old lady picking over the tea towels. Were they real people? Or killers in disguise?

As the Muzak played, John and I headed in opposite directions to scope the place out. Pretending to bargain-hunt, we were actually slipping loaded ammo into various hiding places around the store so later, wherever the action went down in this game, we'd have freshly loaded weapons at our fingertips.

When we finally met up again, John handed me one of the walkie-talkies he'd picked up in the toy department. I showed him the meat-tenderizing tool I'd picked up in kitchenware.

John got distracted by a display of little robotic vacuum cleaners called Roomba, but I managed to drag him away.

And now—we were ready.

Hand in hand, John and I looked for a strong vantage point

from where we could await our enemies, and we soon found the perfect place.

The store's "Prairie Room" included a fake home set on a raised platform, complete with country porch and porch swing. Behind that, a bucolic backdrop of a golden wheat field proclaimed America the Beautiful.

We climbed the steps and sat down on the swing, and discovered that it had a wonderful view of most of the store.

John slipped his arm behind me, and we rocked a little, enjoying the peaceful moment before all hell broke loose.

I could almost imagine that we were an ordinary couple, relaxing on the porch swing after supper while the kids played freeze tag in the yard, squealing when they spotted the first lightning bug of the summer evening . . .

Okay, where did *that* little fantasy come from?

JOHN

Maybe waiting on the porch swing had been a bad idea. Especially with a woman like Jane.

It had my thoughts drifting back to summers long ago, when I was a kid, and the worst thing that could happen was a mosquito bite. I wondered what it would be like to sit on a porch swing every night after supper, watching the sun go down with a girl named Jane . . .

Hell. I told myself I'd better keep my mind on the job or there'd be no more fantasies about anything.

Just in time, too. Someone was watching us. *Stay cool*, I warned myself.

Then we both heard a click. The unmistakable sound of a hammer being cocked. And not the kind of hammer they have in Aisle 3.

We stopped swinging. The whole world seemed to freeze.

I glanced sideways at Jane.

We both knew—this was it.

Calmly we reached into our pockets and pulled on our sunglasses.

"See you in the next life, Jane," I told my wife.

"Likewise, John."

Then—just for extra fun—I hit a button on a handy remote-control device I had in my pocket.

And the lights went out.

JANE

Here we were—the moment of truth. Poised on the edge of our one and only shot. Once we set this in motion, there was no going back. Winner take all.

John and I shared one last look. And in that look I tried to show him everything I felt: hope, sorrow, forgiveness, trust. And love. Most of all, love.

John's smile said he heard me loud and clear, and returned the sentiment. His wink said, *Let's go for it!*

Hell, yeah, I was scared.

But I'd never felt more alive.

I could feel the undercover assassins infiltrating the building. I couldn't see them, but I knew they were there, crawling out of the woodwork like cockroaches.

John's hand on my elbow said, *Move!* And as the lights went out, we leaped out of the porch swing . . . Just in time. Behind us, I heard a soft *thunk! Thunk!*

Within seconds the store erupted into full-blown chaos. We dashed into the house, looking for a back way out. As we passed a playpen filled to the brim with teddy bears, "Homey," the store's life-size mascot, popped out, attired with a house-shaped hat, mustache—and sawed-off shotgun.

Without blinking, we each fired a bullet into his oversize stuffed head. As he fell backward out of the playpen, he fired his shotgun into the ceiling with a startling *boom!*

What had been an undercover skirmish had now escalated into a major public event. Customers screamed, tripping over one another to reach the exits.

Suddenly doors on both sides of the house exploded inward and SWAT teams of assassins poured in from both sides.

Crash! Skylights shattered as a half-dozen killers rappelled down from the roof.

Damn! The whole freakin' army was here!

John and I quickly backtracked through the fake house and out the front door.

When we reached the petunias, we plucked out the smoke grenades we'd hidden like Easter eggs, pulled the pins, and sent them rolling across the floor. The colored smoke made an excellent cover.

We kept ourselves low, and using the panic as a cover, we detoured to the section where bathroom fixtures were sold.

I lifted a toilet seat lid and pulled out my hidden sniper rifle. As I screwed on the barrel, John said, "We gotta draw fire away from the suburbanites. Up or under?"

"I'll fly," I said.

I sprinted for the office section next door, hit the shelves at a dead run, then scaled the fifty feet into the store's rafters with ease as if I were doing a little light rock climbing.

Hanging at the top, I pulled out a pair of night-vision binoculars and looked around . . .

I had a fantastic view of almost the whole layout. The cockroaches were multiplying. I guessed there must be dozens of 'em in the house.

To me, it looked like just about everybody on both sides had shown up—a real family reunion.

I also had a good view of John making his way down a row of refrigerators in kitchen appliances.

And the two assassins waiting at the end of the row.

"Brakes, John!" I squawked into my walkie-talkie. "Nine-o'clock turn!"

John skidded and made a hard left, then disappeared on the other side.

I pulled out my rifle and fired a single clean shot.

Two deadly assassins went down.

John, who'd fired the second shot, stepped back into view and hit his walkie-talkie. "Thanks, hon. Today's my birthday."

"It is?" I exclaimed. Gosh, I thought it was three months from now. "Happy Birthday . . ."

Darn! I hated missing birthdays. I guess saving his life just now was a pretty good present. But if we made it out alive, I swore, I'd make him the best birthday cake ever.

JOHN

Hell, yeah, I was scared. That's part of the job description. But—

Hell, no, I wasn't ready to die. Especially on my birthday.

I sneaked through the store, looking for assassins. Sprinklers showered the floor. It was wet, dark, and freaky in there, almost surreal.

I spotted a trio of assassins combing the furnishings section, scaring shoppers out of their minds.

I let 'em know I was here.

Briiing! Briiing!

I rang the bell on the kids "razor" trike I was

riding and started pedaling as fast as I could. I had a huge gun resting on the little handlebars, and as I streaked down the aisle, the orange flag on the safety pole alerted everyone to where I was, but that's what I wanted.

So we played a game of "now you see him, now you don't" up and down the aisles. Each time I hit an intersection, I fired off a couple of rounds. Then I'd disappear again. Pedal, pursue, fire!

But then I came to a huge intersection where all the lanes converged.

As my flag bobbed out in the open, they fired unmercifully.

But I was way ahead of them. This time the flag wasn't attached to my bike. It was on a shopping cart—filled with propane tanks from the camping section.

Their gunfire caused the tanks to explode. Bye bye, bad guys.

JANE

Making my way through the rafters, I fired off shots whenever I spotted a gun. Problem was, the assassins were still pouring in from everywhere.

Laser sights were scoping out my location. Their light beams crisscrossed over my head like a night at the Oscars. I was seriously outnumbered.

And I'd lost sight of John.

"John?" I called over the walkie-talkie. "Cleanup on Aisle Six. John?"

No answer.

"Shit. You want something done . . ." I complained, not wanting to think of the reasons why he wasn't answering.

I dived over the side, skittering down the shelves like a spider, till I landed in the kids section.

I ditched my spent rifle and felt around on a shelf of stuffed animals.

Still there! A very lethal semiautomatic.

I could've waited for the bad guys to come get me. But I hated waiting. So I took the fight to them.

I spun around a corner and spotted a trio of assassins. We all opened fire, bullets pinging off everything. I took a hit to the shoulder, but it bounced off my body armor.

I spun back around the corner, braced against the wall, breathing hard. Now what?

Just then I heard the roar of an engine. And then *crash!*

A wall of stuffed ninja hamster toys exploded as John came crashing through, straddling one of those monster garden ATV things, complete with trailer. As he skidded to a stop beneath a water sprinkler, it appeared as if he managed to mow down a fair share of the enemy.

"Mean machine, Steve McQueen," I said.

John grinned and held out his hand. I grabbed it and swung up onto the trailer.

John sped away again down the aisles, crashing into merchandise, swerving like a snake so we'd be hard targets to hit.

I reached to pull back the tarp and found a mini-Gatling gun.

John jammed on the brakes and spun the whole vehicle around a hundred and eighty degrees. I didn't ask where he'd learned *that* trick.

Then we drove straight into the gaping jaws of our pursuers.

We charged down the aisle, guns rattling. And fired, round after round. Blowing our assassins into shelves, sending them flying like rag dolls. It was almost too easy—like shooting fish in a barrel.

My God. It looked as if we might actually get out of this alive.

And then this killer comes out of nowhere from behind an inflatable tent.

With a grenade launcher across his broad shoulder. Aimed at us.

Not good.

I didn't even have time to open my mouth and say "Bye, John"—before he fired.

JOHN

Damn!

I gunned the throttle and yanked the steering wheel *hard*—

Inches out of direct fire. But then the rocket grenade exploded right behind us and catapulted us— and our ATV—through a wall.

Which found us back at the Prairie Room, right where we started.

The ATV skidded to a stop and flung us out onto the snowy display, destroying half a dozen Christmas trees.

A soft landing, considering.

We lay there in a heap for a moment, thankful we weren't dead, Jane on top of me. And for a moment, it was just us, alone, in the dark, eerie silence.

"I think our plan's going well," she murmured.

"It is. It is," I said.

But I knew it wasn't over. Not yet.

We leaped up and ran, diving into the metal garden shed, where we'd stashed the bulk of our firepower. We'd even fortified the walls with bags of fertilizer.

Time for Custer's last stand.

Warmed up. We strapped shotguns onto our backs, stuffed more guns into our waistbands and pockets, secured ammo clips, and slid knives onto our shin straps.

I twisted a tourniquet around my wounded arm with my teeth and told Jane it was no big deal.

Suddenly bullets ripped through the hut, slashing holes into the bags of fertilizer.

Next came booted footsteps as our opponents shuffled past us.

Jane crawled forward to peer out of one of the bulletholes.

"How's it look?" I asked.

She took a long, deep breath, then slowly turned back to me with a serene smile on her face. "It's a cinch," she said.

We both knew it was her final lie. "Don't forget," I reminded her. "The Berettas jam up sometimes."

"Got it."

"And you always favor your left, sweetie," I said. "I'll cover right."

"Yeah."

"Bet that boat in La Paz looks pretty good right about now," I said, trying to joke.

But she shrugged. "Rainy season, this time of year." Then she squeezed my hand, all joking aside, and said, "I'm right where I want to be . . ."

I touched her bruised cheek and smiled. "About time . . ."

She looked up at me, her face strong, defiant. She was a true warrior.

My kind of woman. Forever.

We'd said it all.

Now it was time to go.

JANE

It was Butch and Sundance time.

We burst out of the garden shed, armed to the teeth and ready to fight our way out. Or go down trying.

We moved, back-to-back, spinning and firing like two dancers in a well-rehearsed ballet—or like a two-headed killing machine, depending on how you wanted to look at it.

Our assassins dropped like flies.

I tried not to think—only do. One foot in front of the other, one assassin after another, trained movements, steady nerves.

When I ran out of ammo, John slammed in a new clip for me without missing a beat, as if he were an actual extension of me. We moved together, fluid and deadly.

Then I took a hit off my Kevlar, and doubled over. As I caught my breath, John seized the moment to fire the gun strapped to my back. I recovered and went back to work.

Then suddenly I felt John jerk, and go down. Instinctively I dived over him, spinning and shooting in midair, taking out at least a dozen guys.

It was almost as if our whole lives had been leading up to this moment, and God, we were perfect together.

Only then did I realize John had taken a bullet in the leg. As I knelt to see how bad it was, he shook his head indicating that he was okay.

Slowly we got to our feet. Because of his wound, John had to lean on me a little for support.

I liked that.

Then we turned, poised to shoot . . .

And were met with silence.

There was no one left to return our rounds. We had gotten them all. Every damn one of them.

We waited a moment, braced for a last-minute surprise. Wondering if we were only dreaming that it was all over.

But the only sound filling the eerie silence was the sound of our heavy breathing.

It was true. It was all over. And we were both still alive.

With a groan, we let our burning-hot guns drop to the ground. Our eyes locked. Our lips collided.

And we kissed, celebrating our lives right there in the middle of the war zone—as if we were the last two people in the world.

Then a noise woke us from our embrace. We instantly turned, drawing more guns from behind our backs.

Four barrels pointed toward the sound.

But it was only a flaming Mr. HomeMade and several Roombas lurching through the debris.

Dozens of assassins lay dead on the floor as if asleep. Every hired gun in the business, more or less. Atlanta and Father had lost everyone.

Everyone but Mr. and Mrs. Smith.

I wasn't sure where our bosses were. But I knew that somewhere, somehow, they were watching us, tracking everything that had just gone down.

I could imagine their stunned faces. Their shock. Their horror over what this had done to their payrolls, their organizational charts, and their staff.

Both agencies were gonna need a helluva lot of freelance work in the near future.

And I knew a couple of very fine freelancers who might just be available. For a price, of course.

I blinked as we headed into the dazzling sunlight, and thought, *Butch and Sundance, Bonnie and Clyde, Thelma and Louise . . . this one's for you.*

God, it was all over. It was really over! We were free!

And then I turned to John and said what I'd been wanting to say for . . . who knows how long?

"John . . ."

"Yeah?"

"I want a baby."

JOHN

I felt really weird all of a sudden. Kind of like I'd been punched in the gut. Kind of like Superman.

Pretty smart woman, my Jane, coming up with a line like that, here and now.

"I want a baby," she said.

And I knew when I looked at her: I did, too.

Life-and-death situations were just a routine part of my job. But now Jane had changed all that.

Love kind of made you think about things. Like life, death, eternity. And what the hell does it all mean?

Finding Jane again had given me something to live for.

Was I scared by her words? Hell, yeah.

But so what? I made a living out of stuff that would scare most people shitless.

How could babies be harder than that?

"Um, okay, honey," I said softly.

And the smile she gave me made me look forward to keeping my promise.

JANE

Exhausted, streaked with blood and sweat, we strode outside like the Wild Bunch, our weapons still drawn, just in case there were any surprises left.

Shoppers cowered behind cars. Babies cried. Grown men wept. Old ladies prayed.

Suddenly a woman ran out in front of us.

John raised his gun to shoot—

But I touched his arm and shook my head. *It's okay; she's real.*

His jaw clenched; but then, relieved to know it was all over, he lowered his weapon.

I helped him into the van, then climbed in on the driver's side. We were both exhausted, and God, I just wanted to rest for a minute. But sirens began a distant wail and I knew it was time to go.

I looked at my watch. If all had gone according to plan, Atlanta and Father would be tallying their losses—thirty men, at least, on his side; I didn't have time to count how many on her side. That's all of their collective agents on the eastern seaboard. They might even heave a sigh of relief for not calling in their West Coast, London, and Taipei offices. But then they'd be surprised by the unexpected visit of Benjamin Danz, there for what he thinks is a scheduled debriefing. Ah yes, the warning signal on Father's computer would no doubt tip them all off to the existence of an explosive device . . . but would Danz find the credit card John had planted on him in time? I looked at John and felt a sudden tremor. I know he felt it, too.

As I drove out of the parking lot, I covered John's hand with mine, felt the mingling of our sweat and blood.

He smiled at me and laid his head back, his eyelids drooping. I recognized that look; he was fighting sleep. And that was fine with me. He needed the rest, and I was glad to drive my injured hero home.

But . . . home?

Where was that?

Our house had been demolished.

I thought of all the beautiful furniture we'd bought, the knickknacks, the objets d'art. All the boxes in our basement, full of packed, organized, and alphabetized possessions. All gone. Everything was gone.

God, we'd destroyed everything we'd ever built together. Nothing remained.

Where do we go from here?

Just then John whispered my name in his sleep. I looked over with a smile and noticed a huge bulge in his pants pocket.

Not that I was looking.

As he shifted in his seat, I could see the tip of a silver flask jutting out of his pocket. It was the one I'd given him so long ago.

So something did remain after all.

A silver vessel. Something to toast our new life with.

To dodging bullets, I'd had it inscribed. *Love, Jane.*

These magic words whispered into a future we couldn't possibly have imagined.

John and I *had* dodged a lot of bullets together. And not just the ones fired from guns.

We'd dodged a lot of emotional barbs throughout our six-year marriage, too, but we'd lived to talk about it.

And that's when I realized: Our home wasn't destroyed. Our house was. Just a house.

After growing up without a real one, I'd tried to make this one perfect. I'd filled it with possessions that I thought I loved. I guess I brainwashed myself into thinking that perfection meant security, permanence, *love.*

But it was just a house full of things. Nothing that really mattered.

John and I could go anywhere and call it home now. As long as we were together.

I was no longer a naive young newlywed: I knew there'd be a hell of a lot more bullets to dodge in our future—both on and off the job—but we proved we were up for the challenge.

It was going to be a messy, dangerous, unpredictable life.

And I couldn't wait for it to get started.

JOHN

Jane. What an amazing woman.
    We made it.
Another chance . . .
Tomorrow . . .
Zzzzzzzzzzzzzzzzzzzzzzzzzzzzzzz . . .

DR. WEXLER

Ah, yes. A very successful case—the Smiths. See how writing down your feelings can help?

I haven't seen them in a while, but I did get something in the mail from them recently. It was a change-of-address card. I recognized Jane's handwriting. She'd scribbled a little note at the bottom: Dr. Wexler, Thanks for everything. Love, Jane and John Smith.

I sent them a fruit basket as a housewarming present, and a card reminding them that they still had one free session left.

But somehow, I don't suppose they'll be coming back.

If all married couples were like Mr. and Mrs. Smith . . .

Well, I'd be out of a job.

Maybe Eddie does have a sentimental side after all. He was the only agent to skip the shopping spree at HomeMade that day. He also recovered these photos from the rubble that was once the biggest East Coast special-ops center. To hear him tell our story, we're the luckiest couple alive. . . . I'd say we'd have to agree with him.

Here we are, taking a shot at love . . .

and getting lucky.

Even though we got married soon after and moved into a beautiful home with a white picket fence, ours was not your average union.

I had my dark little secrets . . .

And so did he.

Sure we managed to fool the neighbors ...

but fooling a marriage counselor, a friend like Eddie, *and* each other was a little harder than that.

We were both hired assassins whose mission was to kill each other! Our marriage was destined to fail.

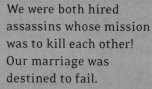

Then this punk set us up... and inadvertently helped us to see the power of our love.

For us, the magic really is in the chase!

We knew we'd have to fight to save our marriage . . . and our careers.

So we traded marriage counseling for a little retail therapy, then shopped until every bad guy dropped.

It looks like the last couple still standing wins!

For Dr. Wexler,
With eternal gratitude for
the oil check.

—Jane and John Smith

ACKNOWLEDGMENTS

This book was a labor of love, as well as a collaborative effort, and so I send my affections and gratitude to all those who helped make this book possible:

To my wonderful editor, Hope Innelli, at HarperCollins, for her encouragement, good humor, and brilliant editorial guidance—and for giving me "hope" when I felt as if I would never finish this book!

To Casey Kait, also at HarperCollins, for her cheerful e-mails and phone calls when deadlines loomed.

To Debbie Olshan, at Twentieth Century Fox, for taking every twist and turn in the adventure with us—I can't wait to see the movie!

To my assistant, Katrina Östlicher—typist extraordinaire and human spellchecker—who spent endless hours compiling my endless notes and transcripts. What would I do without you?

To Cathy, my oldest friend, who is always there for me—thanks for all the late-night sessions!

And last but not least, to Jane and John for sharing their inspiring story. Good luck with all your new adventures, and remember: My door is always open if you ever need to stop by for another "Oil Check."   —M.W.

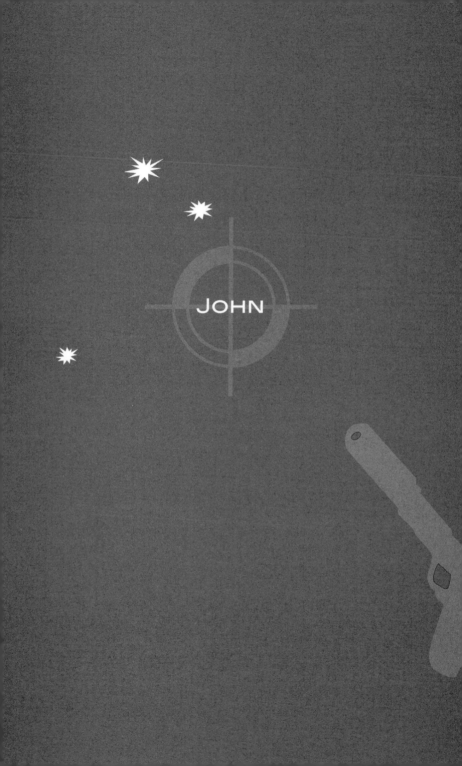